STRATEGIC PLAN

TRIUMPH OVER ADVERSITY

LYNN SHANNON

I can do all this through Him who gives me strength.

4 Philippians 13

ONE

A twig snapped.

Leah Gray whirled. A canopy of tree branches overhead blocked most of the sun, but a few beams of light snuck through. It dappled the walkway through the woods with odd shapes. She peered into the thick brush. No one was there. Still, the hair on the back of her neck rose and goosebumps broke out across her bare arms.

It felt like she was being watched. She'd had that feeling a lot recently.

"Leah." Cassie Miles, her best friend, stood a short distance away on the trail. Her blonde hair was pulled into a ponytail and she'd dressed for the hike in a T-shirt and shorts. "Everything okay?"

The sound of a child's laughter peeled through the woods, followed by slamming doors. Knoxville Nature Park was a popular place with families and hikers. Leah swallowed, the sensation of being watched disappearing in the blink of an eye, leaving her feeling foolish. A flush crept into her cheeks.

"Fine." Leah rolled her shoulders, shaking off the lingering ominous sensation. "I must've heard a squirrel or something. Thank goodness we didn't bring the dogs. Jax would run from here to the other side of the lake, investigating every creature in the area."

Cassie laughed. Jax was Leah's dog. The Lab-mix was fun-loving and goofy, with boundless energy and a love of water. Normally, Leah didn't mind bringing him to the park for a stroll around the lake, but today wasn't a normal day. Her hand tightened on the wreath of flowers as pain slashed her heart.

No, nothing about today was normal. They'd come to honor a fallen friend. A war hero.

Cassie looped her arm through Leah's. They fell into step beside each other, strolling down the worn path toward the lake. The water sparkled in the sunlight, glinting just beyond the trees. A butterfly flitted from a set of wildflowers. Sweat beaded on Leah's brow, aggravated by the oppressive humid air. Texas had many admirable qualities, but summer wasn't one of them.

"Thanks for coming with me this afternoon." Leah adjusted her hold on the wreath. It was covered in flowers and designed to float on the water. "Was Nathan bothered when I said it should just be the two of us?"

Nathan was Cassie's husband. Leah liked him tremendously, but this...this was personal.

"Of course not." Cassie waved a fly away from her face. "Nathan offered to come as a show of support, but it makes sense for you and I to do this alone. We grew up with William."

The four of them—William and his twin sister, Kaylee, Cassie, and Leah—had been inseparable in junior high and high school. All of them had come from troubled families. The dysfunction bonded them together in a way that'd been fundamental. After graduation, William joined the army. He died last year during deployment.

Cassie sighed. "I wish Kaylee were here with us."

"So do I." William's twin sister had disappeared nine months ago, shortly after her brother's death. Leah ducked under a low-hanging branch. "I spoke to the detective in charge of Kaylee's case. He hasn't

2

had any new leads. Probably because he's not doing a thing to find her."

Leah tried to keep the bitterness out of her voice, but it was impossible. The Medina County Sheriff's Department didn't consider Kaylee's disappearance to be a high priority. The detective in charge believed Kaylee had simply left town, a notion Leah adamantly disagreed with.

She feared something terrible had happened to Kaylee.

Leah hounded the sheriff's department with phone calls and in-person visits, attempting to keep the case alive and at the forefront of their minds. To no avail. Unfortunately, in this case, the squeaky wheel didn't always get the grease.

"I drove past the billboard you created on my way out of town yesterday," Cassie said. "It looks great."

"Thanks." Desperate to get some new leads on Kaylee's case, Leah rented space on a billboard near the freeway. It had a photo of Kaylee along with a phone number and a reward amount for any information that brought resolution to the case. "There's a private company running the tip line. Hopefully, something will come of it."

She stepped over a fallen log. This path wasn't used often, because the park rangers didn't clear it regularly. But it led to the most beautiful place on the lake. William's secret fishing spot. Last year, they'd spread his ashes here, as he requested. It seemed a fitting spot to lay the wreath as well.

The trees parted, and the lake appeared. The sun hovered on the horizon, painting the sky with pale yellows, oranges, and soft blues. Clouds dotting the sky were reflected in the water. Boats floated in the distance, too far away to destroy the tranquility or disturb the herons searching for their dinner in the weeds.

Leah sighed with appreciation. "Every time I come out here, I'm reminded why William loved this spot so much."

Cassie nodded. "I know. It's gorgeous." Her lips curved into a smile. "Remember that time you caught a catfish? You cried and insisted he put it back into the water."

She chuckled. "William was so mad. It was a huge catfish. I never fished with bait again after that." Memories pushed at the edges of her mind. William's laugh had been boisterous and wild, his grin infectious, and his humor razor-sharp. Their relationship had never been romantic. It was more like a brother and sister. His death, and the disappearance of Kaylee, tore at Leah. Hot tears filmed her eyes. She blinked rapidly to clear her vision before shoving her glasses higher on her nose. "I miss him. I miss them both."

"Me too."

Cassie embraced her, and they held each other for a long moment. Then Leah cleared her throat. "Okay, let's get this wreath in the water before we're both a sobbing mess."

They each held half of the wreath and stepped closer to the lake. Leah bent so part of the wreath was in the water and then bowed her head. "Dear Lord, thank You for giving us William. We're grateful for all the years we shared with him and the many ways he enriched our lives." Leah pictured William in her mind. "Until we meet again, my friend."

She and Cassie released the wreath. It bobbed on the water, drifting farther out onto the lake, pushed by the gentle current and a faint breeze. The scent of gardenias, the flowers on the wreath, wrapped around them like a comforting embrace. Leah felt the tension of the day ease from her muscles.

Cassie glanced at her watch. "Oh, Leah, I'm sorry. I've got to run or I'm going to be late for my meeting. We have a new horse arriving tonight from West Texas." She ran a horse rehabilitation center. The best in Texas. "Poor thing looks awful in the pictures."

Leah winced. How anyone could abuse an animal, she couldn't fathom. It was far too common and something she saw regularly as the lead administrator for the Knoxville Animal Shelter. "Don't worry, Cass. Thanks for coming with me."

"You don't want to walk back to our cars together?"

"It's so pretty here. I'll stay for a bit and watch the sunset."

"Okay." Cassie started to turn, then paused. "I almost forgot to ask. How did your doctor's appointment go today?"

Leah had spent hours at the hospital, being poked and prodded. No wonder she was emotionally on edge. These tests would determine if her breast cancer was in full remission or if the beast had reared its ugly head to take another bite at her. She didn't want to think about it. "The results should be in next week. For now, we just wait."

"I'll be praying for you." Cassie gave her one last hug before hurrying up the trail. Her slender form disappeared behind the tree branches.

A collection of rocks jutted into the lake from the shoreline. Leah used one as a chair, propping her legs up on another. Sweat dripped down her back. Judging from the waning sunlight, it would be twilight soon. Mosquitoes droned, hovering at the lake edge, but didn't bother her. Leah had doused herself with an obscene amount of bug spray before venturing into the woods.

Silence embraced her. The wreath was a faint dot on the water. A blue-gray heron stretched its long neck above the weeds along the shoreline before taking flight. The giant bird was a beauty to behold. Leah let her gaze follow it across the lake, contentment seeping into her pores. She loved the peacefulness of nature.

A bush rustled behind her. Leah turned, half expecting a woodland creature to emerge from the tree line. A squirrel or maybe even an otter. Her pulse skittered as a very different kind of animal stepped free of the branches.

A man wearing a pig mask.

She froze, shock rendering her muscles useless as her mind tried to process what was happening. Was this some kind of joke? A foolish individual looking to scare someone alone on the lake? Her ears strained to hear the sound of anyone else on the trail behind the masked man. A group of friends, witness to the horrible prank, maybe filming it for social media.

Nothing. There was no one behind the man.

He stepped closer and something inside Leah snapped into crisp clarity. This wasn't a joke. He meant her harm.

Run!

She bolted from the set of rocks, her tennis shoes sliding in the mud along the water's edge. Going back up the path toward the parking lot wasn't possible. The masked man was blocking it. Instead, Leah ran along the coastline. Weeds grabbed at her ankles and low-hanging tree branches threatened to smack her in the face. Footsteps pounded behind her, striking terror in her heart.

He was coming for her. To catch her.

And then...only God knew what he would do to her.

Leah screamed.

TWO

A blood-curdling scream echoed across the lake.

Tucker Colburn jerked his head up, searching for the source of the horrific sound. His boat bobbed in the water. The shoreline was a mass of thick tree branches and overgrown brush. A flock of birds took flight from a nearby copse of pines. Crows. Their black-winged bodies flew over his head, the sight ominous and foreboding.

Silence followed. Nothing appeared amiss. Had it been a bird? Or maybe some other animal? Tucker wasn't a country boy. He'd been born and raised in Boston, more accustomed to the concrete sidewalks and constant hustle of people than the gentle lapping of the lake and the sounds of wildlife. Didn't this area of Texas have bobcats? He vaguely remembered reading something about that while visiting the Boston Zoo as a kid.

A mosquito whined in his ear, and Tucker smacked at it. The pesky bugs were out in droves. William hadn't mentioned that part when he described the beauty of Lake Knoxville. The rest though... he'd been right. It was gorgeous here. A beautiful sunset painted the sky with shades of blues and pinks. The water was still and flat, reflecting the beauty of the clouds on the surface. Tucker had motored around the entire shore in his small dingy before finally drifting to a stop in one of the lagoons. It was quiet and secluded. Perfect.

He reached into the backpack at his feet and pulled out a wooden box. An eagle decorated the lid alongside the insignia of the 75th Ranger Regiment. William and Tucker had both been members of the elite special forces unit, better known as Army Rangers. They'd gone through training, were deployed overseas, and completed numerous missions together.

Only one of them made it back stateside alive.

He lifted the lid of the box. Inside, there were two items. One was a necklace on a thick silver chain. It had a pendant. The image of Christ on a cross, complete with a crown of thorns, was formed in the metal. William had worn it every day underneath his shirt.

Tucker brushed his fingers across the necklace before picking up the other item in the box. A photograph. William, dark hair mussed, wearing a broad grin, had his arm thrown over the shoulders of a woman. His twin, Kaylee. She was several inches shorter than her brother, but shared his olive skin and crooked smile. Blood stained the corner of the picture.

William's blood.

Tucker shut his eyes as memories threatened to overwhelm his senses. His heart picked up speed. He'd failed his comrade. His friend. William had died half a world away from a gunshot wound, clutching his necklace in one hand and Tucker's shirt in the other.

Promise me. Promise you'll take care of Kaylee. Take her the necklace and the photo. Tell her...tell her I'm sorry. And that I love her.

It'd been one year since he'd pledged that oath, but Tucker hadn't been able to fulfill his promise. He'd returned stateside five months after William's death, his enlistment with the Army coming to a close. His age, along with the number of injuries he'd received during his years in the military, left him battle-scarred. William's death had driven home the frayed emotional state Tucker was in. He was a danger to himself and to his unit. It was time to get out.

Shortly thereafter, he'd arrived in Knoxville to find Kaylee. But William's twin was gone. Technically, Kaylee was listed as a missing person, but the police believed she'd left town and would pop back up one day. It put Tucker in a strange limbo. He had no real home anymore—not since his dad died five years ago—so staying in Knoxville was the same as any other place in the US. He'd wait for Kaylee's return.

He owed William that much. The man had saved his life.

Another scream rent the air. Tucker jolted, his fingers crumpling the picture in his hand, even as his gaze scanned the shoreline. This time the sound had been closer and easier to distinguish. Was it from a woman? It'd sounded frantic and piercing. And terrified.

Or was he losing his mind? It was a horrifying thought. He'd had flashbacks and minor panic attacks. Both were common among veterans adjusting to civilian life. War changed a person fundamentally, but he was fortunate to have a group of new friends nearby who understood the challenges. A group of fellow veterans from all branches of the military who met every week to support each other. Tucker hadn't shared his real reason for being in Knoxville with them yet. William's death was too raw, too painful, to discuss.

He shifted on the plank seat in his boat, but there was no sign of anyone. The sun was setting quickly, the woods disappearing into dark shadows. A fish jumped before splashing back into the depths of the lake. Mosquitoes encircled his head like bombers seeking a target. If Tucker had imagined that scream, it would be a first.

What if he wasn't imagining it? What if there was a woman in trouble?

Tucker placed the picture back into the box, alongside the necklace, and slammed the lid shut before shoving it back into his backpack. Then he fired up the motor on his dingy. It was hard to pinpoint the origin of the scream, since sounds on the lake echoed, but if Tucker were to hazard a guess, it'd come from around the bend.

The boat shot forward as he increased his speed. Air blew through the thin fabric of his T-shirt, cooling the sweat coating his skin. He kept his gaze on the shoreline as he exited the lagoon.

There.

A woman raced along the edge of the lake. Her clothes were spotted with mud, as if she'd fallen and gotten back up. Curly hair bounced with every step. Tucker was too far away to make out her facial features, but her complexion was beet red, as if she'd been running for miles. She cast a glance over her shoulder. Tucker's heart rate kicked up a notch as he registered the man chasing her. If there was any doubt about the woman being the source of the screams, it was extinguished immediately.

The guy was wearing a pig mask.

"Hey!" Tucker yelled, but his voice didn't carry across the wide distance of the lake. With horror he watched the masked man tackle the woman. They tussled and then the attacker got the upper hand. He shoved her face in the water.

He was going to drown her.

Holding the boat's rudder with one hand, Tucker yanked his handgun from its holster. A decade in the military had taught him an appreciation and respect for weapons. It'd also prepared him to antic-ipate the worst in people. Tucker rarely went anywhere without his gun or the K-Bar knife strapped to his ankle. Not that he couldn't handle himself in hand-to-hand combat. But that was always a last resort.

Taking aim and holding his breath, he fired. The bullet missed its mark—shooting from a moving boat across such a wide distance was more difficult than it appeared in television shows—but it was enough to get the criminal's attention. Pig man released the woman and bolted for the trees. Tucker couldn't stop him. He was too far away.

Instead, he put his focus on the woman still in the water. Was she moving?

Come on, come on.

The boat's engine was designed for a leisurely cruise of the lake, not a race to the shoreline. It wheezed, struggling to work at the maximum setting Tucker demanded. Every second felt like an eternity. His chest clamped tight.

Tucker refused to allow another person to die on his watch. It couldn't happen.

Finally, his boat reached shore. Tucker killed the engine and hopped into the water, pausing only long enough to shove the dinghy onto enough dry land that it wouldn't drift back out into the lake. If the woman was injured, which was likely given the horrendous attack, then the boat was the fastest way to get medical help. Tucker gripped his gun as he sledged through the hip deep water toward the woman. His gaze shot to the trees. Would the masked man return? Or was he still there? It was possible.

He swallowed hard as the woman came into view. She floated in the reeds, face-down. Not moving. Curly hair waved around her head, the bare skin of her arms bone white against the murky water. Tucker grabbed her shoulder to flip her over.

A hand shot out punching him square in the jaw. He reared back, nearly slipping in his haste to avoid the second fist coming for his nose. It bounced off his shoulder. Tucker raised his hands, but the woman kept coming. Screaming, clawing, punching. He couldn't get out of range. Desperately, he grabbed her wrist with one hand, blocking the next hit with his arm.

"I'm here to help." She didn't seem to register his words, her movements becoming frantic. Another hit bounced off his torso. It didn't hurt, but the terrified expression etched across her features was a gut-punch. With a sudden zip of realization, Tucker recognized her. "Leah. It's Tucker Colburn. I'm helping you."

She paused, fist raised to hit him again. Leah blinked. Wet hair clung to her face and neck. The T-shirt and shorts encasing her slender form were soaked. They didn't know each other well, had only met a few times through friends. Tucker doubted she could see him clearly—Leah had once joked she was blind without her glasses —so he spoke again. "It's me, Leah. Tucker. You're safe. I've got you."

Leah gradually lowered her fist. Angry red marks covered her throat and her chest heaved with the force of her fighting efforts. "Tucker."

Her voice came out raw and ragged. She swayed. Tucker wrapped his arm around her waist, hauling her against him to keep her steady. He towered over her, his 6'2 frame at least eight to nine inches bigger than hers. The scent of the lake surrounded them, but the fragrance of lavender wafted from her wet hair.

An itch between his shoulder blades drove his head up and his attention back to the woods. Tucker tightened his hold on his gun.

Someone was hidden in the trees. Watching them.

THREE

Red and blue lights strobed across the parking lot. Leah tugged the emergency blanket more tightly around her shoulders. She couldn't get warm. Night had fallen, bringing with it cooler temperatures, and her clothes were soaked. Or maybe it was the memory of the assault that left her chilled to the core. She'd barely survived the vicious attack. A shudder rippled through her body.

Her gaze drifted across the squad cars in the parking lot before landing on Tucker. He stood a short distance away, speaking to a Medina County deputy. His shirt was still damp from helping Leah from the water. The fabric clung to every curve and dip of his powerful muscles. He wore cargo shorts and flip-flops. An auburn beard covered his jaw, drawing attention to the curve of his lips and the hard line of his nose.

Leah didn't know Tucker well. He was close with Cassie's husband, Nathan, so they'd met a handful of times at various functions. She'd pegged Tucker as the quintessential strong and silent type. He'd barely said half a dozen sentences in her presence. Still, she ferreted out a few nuggets of information about him. Tucker had served in the military—although Leah didn't know what branch—

and didn't have any family in the area. He currently attended university classes in Austin, mostly online, and rented a small house near the lake. He was also single. Cassie had dropped that last piece of info more than once, but Leah had the vague feeling Tucker considered her flighty and vapid. He'd never shown any interest in her.

Tucker said one last thing to the deputy before turning and crossing the parking lot on long strides toward Leah. His legs were the size of tree trunks, but his steps were surprisingly quiet. The memory of being held against him flashed in her mind, and to Leah's horror, her cheeks heated. She smashed down the errant attraction. It'd been years since a man had held her in his arms. Not since her boyfriend broke up with her shortly after Leah was diagnosed with cancer.

The mere thought of her ex was enough to chase away any notions of romance from her mind. Still, Tucker's gaze was as potent as a touch. Leah self-consciously shoved a wild curl behind her ear with one hand and gripped the emergency blanket with the other as he came to a stop in front of her.

"Are you okay?" His voice was gruff. Tucker's attention drifted to her throat and his mouth flattened. "Your throat is bruised pretty badly. Why didn't they take you to the hospital?"

"EMS offered. I refused." The bout with cancer had left a sour taste in her mouth regarding clinics. She was grateful to the doctors and other medical professionals that'd saved her life, absolutely, but undergoing exams and tests caused anxiety. Leah didn't like feeling helpless. Her hand drifted to her neck. "It looks worse than it is."

Her throat was raw from being strangled and bruises were welling up on various parts of her body, but it paled compared to the emotional trauma of the attack. The assailant had chased her for half a mile. Caught her once and began beating her. Leah escaped, only to be captured a second time, before being choked and held underwater. She'd initially fought him, and then in desperation, played dead.

Would it have worked? She didn't know. Tucker had interrupted the attack, thank God.

Fresh goosebumps rippled across her bare legs. She shifted uncomfortably in soggy tennis shoes. "Thank you, Tucker. You saved my life."

"I'm glad you're okay." His lips tilted upward into the hint of a smile before shoving his hands into the pockets of his cargo shorts. Awkward silence descended between them for several beats. Then Tucker tilted his head, a crease forming between his brows. "The police located your glasses?"

She automatically adjusted the black-rimmed frames. "No. I have spare sets everywhere. These are from my car." Leah sighed, dropping her hand. "They took my initial statement but asked me to wait for the detective."

"Same."

Tucker turned and joined Leah in leaning against her SUV. The scent of lake water wafted from his clothes, but underneath was a hint of cologne. Sandalwood and musk. Distinctly masculine. Leah resisted the urge to study her reflection in a nearby vehicle. She'd survived a near-death attack, for crying out loud. What difference did it make if her hair was a wild rat's nest or mascara had run all over her face?

A man stepped out of the woods on the other side of the parking lot, several deputies trailing behind him. Detective Derrick Walsh. Leah's muscles instinctively tensed as a wash of anger flooded her veins. Tucker must've sensed her tension, because he pushed off the SUV, his gaze sweeping the parking lot. "What is it?"

"The detective. I know him."

Before Leah could say more, Detective Walsh was within earshot. Mid-forties, his blond hair was speckled with gray and thinning, but he kept in shape with some outdoor activity that also tanned his skin a deep tawny color. He wore a suit despite the muggy weather. The jacket opened slightly, revealing his holster and gun.

Detective Walsh met her heated gaze with his usual smirk. "Ms. Gray, we meet again."

He made it sound like they were at a party instead of a crime scene. Leah jutted up her chin. "I was attacked." Her stomach roiled as the horror of the experience sank into her. "Targeted."

Tucker's gaze shot to her, but he remained quiet. Detective Walsh, however, frowned. "My deputies filled me in on the attack, and while I'm sorry you had to go through that, there's nothing in their report to indicate you were specifically targeted."

She battled to keep her voice calm. "I've had the feeling someone has been following me for the last few days. I mentioned it to the deputy who took my statement."

"But you've never seen anyone?"

"No." Leah blew out a breath, knowing her next words wouldn't land well. "I think the attack has something to do with Kaylee's disappearance."

"Kaylee?" Tucker interjected. "Kaylee Ross?"

Surprise flickered through Leah, drawing her attention to the man standing at her side. Tucker's expression was hard. The red-and-blue strobe lights from the police vehicles played along the rugged edges of his features. She frowned. "Yes, Kaylee Ross. We went to school together. She's one of my best friends. How do you know her?"

"I don't. At least, not exactly. I served with her brother, William."

Her mouth dropped open. "You're an Army Ranger?"

"Was an Army Ranger, yeah. I—"

"As much as I love listening to this conversation, I have real work to do." Detective Walsh rocked back on the heels of his expensive loafers. "Ms. Gray, I understand you want answers about Kaylee's disappearance, but that doesn't mean this incident is connected."

Leah tugged the emergency blanket off her shoulders and crumpled it into a ball. "I rented a billboard last week near the freeway. It has Kaylee's picture, the details about her disappearance, and a tipline number. There's also a reward for any information that solves the case."

Derrick's expression soured. "You did what?"

"You heard me. I've told you and others at the sheriff's department over and over that Kaylee wouldn't have left town without saying anything."

Anger pulsed through her veins. She'd fought for months to get someone in the sheriff's department to listen to her. Leah had even reached out to Chief Garcia with the Knoxville Police Department. He'd been receptive to her concerns, but Kaylee's disappearance was outside his jurisdiction. He couldn't investigate. She'd been desperate for answers, and given tonight's attack, Leah's concern about Kaylee's disappearance was valid.

Her hand tightened on the blanket. "Within a day of the billboard going up, it felt like someone was watching me. I dismissed my intuition, convinced myself that I was imagining things. But I didn't conjure up the guy in the pig mask. He's real. And he nearly killed me."

Her impassioned speech seemed to have no effect on Derrick. He clicked his pen closed. "Ms. Gray, I have to work on facts. Right now, there's nothing to indicate tonight's attack is connected to Kaylee's disappearance. The billboard could be a coincidence." He arched his brows. "As much as it pains me to say this, women have been attacked on the trails before. That's why law enforcement often advises the buddy system whenever individuals utilize the park."

Tucker stood like a silent sentry, his stance wide, arms crossed over his chest. Whatever he was thinking was hidden behind an expressionless mask. Did he think she was as crazy as Detective Walsh? Frustration bubbled inside Leah. She was normally an even-tempered individual, but Derrick rubbed her the wrong way. Actually, the entire sheriff's department hadn't taken her concerns seriously.

What did that mean for Kaylee? No one was looking for her, and that fact terrified Leah.

Arguing with the detective wouldn't help, but Leah couldn't let it go either. She sucked in a deep breath to temper her emotions and let it out slowly. "Please, Detective Walsh, I'm begging you. Take another look at Kaylee's case. I understand you have to keep an open mind, but it's a strange coincidence that I was attacked so soon after the billboard went up."

His expression softened and a flash of sympathy darkened his eyes. "Ms. Gray, I assure you, we investigate all matters thoroughly. Kaylee's officially classified as a missing person and her case is still active. If any new leads develop, we will follow up." He paused. "On a personal note, I know you're worried about Kaylee. It may seem strange to you, but it's not uncommon for adults to take off without telling friends or family, only to return months or years later. I've seen it many times in my career."

His mind was made up. Leah was wasting her breath. Continuing the conversation would only make things worse and shred the last of her nerves.

Derrick tucked his pad and pen back into his coat pocket. "You're both free to go. I'll contact you with updates on the case." He eyed Leah. "Would you like a ride home? I can have a deputy drive you."

"No, I'll be fine. Thanks."

He strolled away. Leah watched him go, heart in her throat and stomach churning. She was exhausted and injured but refused to let Detective Walsh determine whether or not Kaylee's case should be taken seriously.

This wasn't over. Far from it.

Tucker cleared his throat. "It's late. Why don't I drive you home?"

Leah opened her driver's side door with a jerk and tossed the blanket inside. "No need. I can drive myself."

His hand landed on hers. The warmth of his touch shocked her, and Leah stilled. She swung her gaze to meet his. Tucker's eyes were hard flints of green shamrock, but there was no tension in his fingers. Whatever anger was brewing under the surface, it wasn't directed at her.

"You've been through an ordeal, and although you seem fine at the moment, it's the adrenaline. It's a bad idea to drive yourself. Please, Leah, let me take you."

FOUR

He didn't know what to believe.

Tucker gripped the steering wheel with one hand, his mind churning as quickly as the tires of his old pickup truck. He'd bought it second-hand after leaving the military. It had a dent or two in the body, but the engine was solid and the interior spotless. Headlights illuminated the dark country road. The scent of lake water and mud filled the cab, and he'd lowered the window just enough to allow some fresh air to blow in. In the passenger seat beside him, Leah worried her bottom lip. She hadn't said much since accepting his offer to drive her home.

A thousand questions tumbled through his brain. Was Kaylee truly in trouble? Or was the detective right and she'd disappeared from her regular life for a while? Either was a possibility. Kaylee taking off without telling Leah wasn't enough to cause serious concern. Sometimes people kept their true feelings closely guarded. Especially if they thought someone they cared about would disapprove. Before tonight, Tucker had taken Detective Walsh's theory about the case at face value.

Maybe that'd been a mistake. Tonight's attack raised serious questions about Kaylee's disappearance, and Tucker needed to know more, but he held back. So far, Leah had kept it together, but she'd been through a traumatic experience. He didn't want to push her beyond what she could handle.

Her curls fluttered in the slight breeze coming from the open window. They were the color of walnuts, unruly and wild. Tucker kept a spare hoodie in the car, and he'd given it to Leah, since her clothes were still damp. It swallowed her petite frame, making her seem more vulnerable and fragile. Fingerprint bruises marred the delicate skin at her throat. The sight of them sent a fresh dose of anger through Tucker's veins. If he hadn't been on the lake tonight...

She'd be dead.

He gripped the steering wheel harder, his knuckles turning white with the effort. No woman should be terrorized. That was a fact. But the idea that Leah had been specifically targeted worried him deeply.

"Slow down," Leah said, cutting into his thoughts. "The turn into my neighborhood is just ahead."

He did as she instructed and, moments later, pulled into the driveway of a small one-story. A large oak tree shaded the front yard and a wild riot of flowers burst from brick-lined beds. Tucker hopped out of his truck and circled the vehicle to the passenger side. His gaze scanned the neighborhood for any potential threat, but found none.

He opened Leah's door and stepped back so she could exit. She pulled a set of keys from her pocket. "I know it's late, but you're welcome to come inside." Her mouth tilted up at the corners, although the smile didn't erase the worry buried in her eyes. "I've got a cherry pie from Nelson's Diner and there's a tub of vanilla ice cream in my freezer to go with it."

Leah didn't want to be alone; that much was obvious. Tucker didn't need her to explain why. He shut the vehicle door and grinned broadly. "You said the magic words. I never turn down pie from Nelson's." The diner was famous for their dessert. Tucker and his fellow veterans met there every Wednesday for dinner.

He followed her up the walkway. When Leah unlocked her front door, dogs began barking. One was yappy and high-pitched, the other slower and much deeper. She pushed inside, ordering the animals to sit. One dog was a Lab-mix, with white patches splayed across his black coat. His ear was clipped and it appeared he was blind in his left eye. The other pup was teeny with dark brown fur and giant eyes. Her entire body wriggled with excitement, although she stayed seated as ordered by her mistress.

Leah gestured to the small one first. "That's Coconut. She's a mini-Chihuahua." Then she pointed to the other mutt, sitting politely at the edge of the kitchen. "And that's Jax."

Tucker removed his soggy shoes and socks to avoid tracking lake water over her floor and set them by the door. Then he allowed each dog to sniff his hand before petting them. "They're sweet. What happened to Jax's eye and ear?"

"I'm not sure." Leah tossed him a glance over her shoulder as she fished doggie treats from a canister on the kitchen counter. "Jax and Coconut were abandoned at different times and ended up rooming together at the shelter. They bonded, and no one wanted to adopt them together, so I brought them home."

Leah was the head administrator for the Knoxville Animal Shelter. It was sweet of her to adopt the dogs together. The act was proof of her soft heart and giving nature, something Tucker had noticed about her right away. She was also quirky and fun-loving. Before today, he'd never seen her worried or stressed. Leah showed up everywhere with a smile, and although she was stunningly gorgeous, Tucker refused to allow the spark of interest between them to develop into something more. He was far too quiet and reserved for someone like Leah. Too much like his old man.

Matrimonial bliss hadn't worked out for Pop. Tucker figured it wouldn't end much better for him, so better to skip the entire thing to begin with. Bachelor life was simple. It suited him.

Tucker cleaned up in Leah's washroom as best he could, considering his unexpected dip in the lake. Feeling better, he went back into the kitchen. A cat meandered in, weaving its way through Tucker's feet before greeting Leah who was coming out of the back bedroom. She must've taken the fastest shower in history, because her hair was damp, the mud was gone from her legs, and she'd changed into fresh clothes.

Leah scratched the cat's ears while offering Tucker a smile. "Give me a few minutes and dessert will be ready."

"Take your time." He wandered into the next room. Several bird cages sat next to a window. One held a Macaw, the other a few smaller birds Tucker couldn't name. Another cage held a fuzzy ball tucked into a hammock. Tucker frowned. "Is that a squirrel?"

"Chinchilla. Her name is Lola." Leah pulled ice cream out of the freezer. She was visible through the cutout over the bar separating the kitchen from the rest of the living space. "I have a lot of pets, I know. All of them are foundlings. Most were dropped off at the shelter, like Lola. Someone dumped her in a cat carrier outside before opening hours. The shelter only houses cats and dogs, so she didn't have anywhere to go. I posted Lola on social media, searching for a forever home but didn't get any takers." Leah grinned, her whole face lighting up. "So now she's mine."

Tucker nodded, his gaze drifting around the rest of the space. It was modest but packed with color. The walls were a golden yellow, the couch a deep blue, and the accent chair orange. Leah had made good use of the space by eliminating a formal dining room and using it to house her birds and chinchilla. Dog beds, one tiny and one extra-large, were also in the room. Novels overflowed from a nearby bookshelf to rest on the floor in stacks. The effect was comfortable. Lived-in. Homey.

It was a stark contrast to Tucker's own apartment across town. The only pieces of furniture were his bed, a second-hand couch, a card table and folding chair. He ate on paper plates. The most expensive things he owned were his truck and the computer he'd bought for college. A decade in the military had taught him to live lightly, and nine months as a civilian hadn't erased the tendency.

Leah set two plates on the bar, each with a thick slice of cherry pie and a generous scoop of ice cream. Tucker eyed the stool and debated whether it was strong enough to hold his weight before deciding to forgo it and stand. He picked up his fork and was about to dig in when he noticed Leah was praying. He politely waited for her to finish. To his relief, Leah didn't ask why he didn't join in. She must've noticed during the few meals they'd shared among friends that he didn't pray.

His faith—or lack thereof—wasn't something he wanted to discuss.

Tucker cut into the flaky crust and scooped it into his mouth. Flavor exploded across his tastebuds. The tartness of the pie was the perfect combination for the sweet vanilla ice cream. He took another few bites, before glancing at Leah out of the corner of his eye. She was quiet again. Worry seemed to seep off her muscles.

Tucker inwardly groaned. He'd never been skilled at making small talk, but he'd come into Leah's home to make her feel more secure, not to eat her pie. He swiped his mouth with a napkin. "This is good."

"It is." Leah swirled her fork around in the white puddle forming under her melting ice cream. "Were you at the lake today because of William? It's the anniversary of the day he died."

The dessert curdled in his stomach. William was another topic Tucker didn't want to discuss, but it was unavoidable. "Yes, I was on the lake because of William. He told me about his favorite fishing spot. I was hoping to find it."

"You were close. It was in the next cove, around the bend." She pushed aside her half-eaten pie. "That's why I was there too. Cassie and I went to lay a wreath on the water. She had to leave, and I stayed behind. I wanted a few moments to think about him..." Her voice choked off.

Grief, hot and unexpected, swelled inside Tucker. He battled it back. Now wasn't the time. Since Leah had brought up the subject, it was a good opportunity to gauge the validity of her concerns about Kaylee's disappearance. "Were you and William close? He talked about a few friends back home, but never mentioned your name."

She swiped at a tear coursing down her cheek. "No, he wouldn't have. William always called me by my real first name, Lenora." She wrinkled her nose. "I hate it. He did it to tease me."

Tucker's mouth dropped open. "You're Lenora?" William had chewed his ear off about his high school friends. A band of misfits, but closer than blood. Something inside of Tucker twisted hard. "All this time...I had no idea."

"There was no way for you to." She sniffed and ripped off a paper towel before swiping under her nose. Then her gaze hardened as she lifted it to meet Tucker's. "I have a confession. I didn't only invite you in for pie. I need your help."

"To find Kaylee?"

"Yes. The attack tonight wasn't a coincidence. I'm convinced it's connected to my search for Kaylee. I'm scared for her. She wouldn't have just disappeared from town without telling me, no matter what Detective Walsh thinks." Leah tilted her head, assessing him. "If William told you about his life here in Knoxville, then you understand how close we all were."

Tucker nodded, but the knot of uncertainty churning his stomach wouldn't abate. Kaylee and Leah might've been very close —as William had attested—but people kept secrets. They changed. Leah believed Kaylee's disappearance was suspicious, but that didn't make it so. He needed more information. "What do you know—"

Coconut erupted in barking, and Jax lumbered to his feet to join her. Tucker's gaze shot to the back door. "Are you expecting someone?"

Leah's complexion paled and a hand went to her throat. The

bruises had darkened to a purple. She shrank back from the door. "No. Especially not at this hour."

It was close to midnight. Far too late for the average caller. It would be a risk for Leah's attacker to show up at her home, but the man hadn't had a problem chasing her in a public park. He was bold and ruthless.

"Stay here." Tucker placed his hand on his gun but kept it holstered. The dogs' barking grew more frantic. He eased around the corner of the bar into the kitchen. His gaze was locked on the back doorknob.

It slowly turned.

FIVE

Leah's heart thundered in her ears. The urge to run and hide warred with an instinct to protect her home. The dogs barking had escalated to a frantic level. Tucker, his broad shoulders rigid, kept his hand on the gun holstered in the back of his pants.

The door swung open.

A woman wearing a miniskirt and high heels stood on the porch. It was Mimi Olsen, Leah's mother. Her frizzy hair was dyed a bleach blonde and curled. Makeup was smeared across her face, giving her a clown-like appearance. A sparkly purse was askew on her shoulder. Mimi swayed on the doorstep before leaning heavily on the doorframe.

Leah's knees went weak with relief, even as a flash of irritation bolted through her. "Mom, what are you doing?" She skirted around Tucker. A blast of vodka and cigarette smoke coming from her mother's direction made her wince. "Your house is next door."

"Can't seem to find the doggone key." Mimi tottered inside. "Cory and I got into an argument down at the Backyard Bar. Told him I was coming here for tonight. I'm lettin' him cool off a spell."

Leah smothered a sigh. It wasn't the first time her mother and stepfather, Cory, had gotten into a public altercation. Some had even become violent, although her mother refused to leave the man. When Leah bought her house, the garage had already been converted into an apartment. She'd given her mom the key so Mimi would have a place to crash if things got bad between her and Cory. "How did you get here? You didn't drive, did you?"

"Stop lecturing me. I took a taxi." Mimi frowned. "You're such a buzzkill."

Leah smothered a sharp retort. Mimi had a way of pushing every one of her buttons. She'd never been a conventional mother, but since meeting Cory, she'd turned into someone Leah didn't recognize. It was painful and heartbreaking.

Mimi drew up short as her bloodshot eyes registered Tucker who was still standing in the kitchen. "Who are you?" She lifted thin brows before cackling. "Oh Leah, are you on a date?"

"No."

The word came out forcefully. She took her mother's arm and attempted to steer her back toward the door. Leah was desperate to avoid a scene that'd played out more than once. But Mimi slipped her grasp and, faster than her drunk stagger would indicate, closed the distance to Tucker. The dogs scampered to get out of her way. They always kept a leery distance from Mimi when she was intoxicated.

She placed a hand on the center of his chest and batted her mascara-coated eyes. "Hey, handsome, what's your name?"

Leah wanted the floor to swallow her whole. Her cheeks heated with shame and embarrassment. Tonight had been terrifying, and the last thing she had patience for was her drunk mother. She crossed her arms over her chest. "Enough, Mom. Let's go."

Mimi didn't budge. She fingered a button on Tucker's shirt with a long acrylic nail, her gaze never leaving Tucker's face. "There's no need to be rude, hon. I'm introducing myself to the man." She flashed what was supposed to be a flirty smile. "I'm Mimi."

Tucker's gaze flickered to meet Leah's for a brief moment. A glimpse of pity flashed across his handsome features before he focused back on Mimi. He gently removed her hand from his chest, took a step back, and shook it. "My name is Tucker Colburn, ma'am. It's nice to meet you."

"Oooo, a real gentleman." Mimi flashed a dark look toward Leah. "Haven't I told you a hundred times to call me Mimi? Mom makes me feel so...old." She shook her head, sending her earrings bobbing. "Leah may be my daughter, but I was sixteen when she was born. Practically a baby. How old are you, Tucker? Good-looking guy like you must get a lot of attention from the ladies."

"Okay, that's it." Leah marched across the kitchen, snagged her mom by the arm, and pulled her toward the front door. "It's late, *Mom*." She put emphasis on the word, hoping it would remind Mimi of her obligations. A futile move. Leah's cancer diagnosis hadn't shocked her mother into being more...well, motherly. Their relationship had always been like sisters—Leah being the more responsible one.

It was exhausting. She was so tired of being on her own.

Leah flung the front door open with the intention of escorting her mother to the garage apartment. A taxi sat in the driveway. Cory climbed out of the back seat, his bald head gleaming in the moonlight. He wore a Western-style shirt and tight jeans held in place by a large belt buckle. Something of a gym rat, he had the physique of a much younger man. Cory owned and operated a junkyard on the far side of town.

What he saw in Leah's mother, she couldn't say but suspected it had something to do with the inheritance checks Mimi received each month. Mimi's mother—Leah's grandmother—had set up a trust for each of them before she died. The steady income had put Leah through college, but unfortunately, it also supported Mimi's destructive lifestyle.

Cory spotted them on the porch and his brows drew down in a scowl. "Mimi, what in tarnation are you doing, woman?"

His words came out slurred. He was also drunk. At least Cory, like Mimi, had the wisdom to take a taxi across town to Leah's house instead of driving himself. Something she was grateful for. It was one thing for her stepfather and mother to be foolhardy with their own lives, quite another to be reckless with innocent people on the road.

"Don't you dare come over here and start hollering at me." Mimi ripped her arm away from Leah's hold and teetered down the porch stairs on her high heels. Her voice soared with rage. "You two-timing good-for-nothing. I saw you dancing with Debbie Wallace."

Leah pursued her mother down the driveway. She'd seen this argument before and knew it could go two ways—one of them physical. She stopped short of interjecting herself between the couple. Tucker joined her. "Do we need to call the police?"

Leah was horribly embarrassed by the question, but it was valid. "Not yet."

Cory pasted on a broad smile. "Darlin', now you know Debbie doesn't hold a candle to you. I can't live without you." He opened his arms wide. "Come on, sweetie. Let's go home."

Like that, the argument was over. Mimi hurried down the driveway toward the taxi but then seemed to remember Leah. She turned around and started back.

Leah met her halfway. Mimi threw her arms open wide and embraced her with gusto. Tears stung the backs of Leah's eyes as a rush of emotion overwhelmed her. Their relationship was complicated, but deep inside, Leah knew her mother loved her. She hugged Mimi back. "You don't have to go with him if you don't want to."

Mimi pulled away before cupping Leah's face. "Don't be silly, sweetie. He's my husband." Her gaze drifted to Tucker, still standing in the driveway. "He's a cutie. Try not to mess things up."

Leah snorted. All her dirty laundry had been waved in front of

Tucker's face. It was a miracle the man wasn't running away from the house screaming. "Pretty sure that ship has sailed, Mom."

"Mimi, get moving." Cory shouted from inside the taxi. "The meter's running."

Leah wrapped her arms around her midsection as her mom teetered to the taxi. She slid into the vehicle and the door slammed shut. Before the taxi backed out of the driveway, Leah met Cory's gaze. He glared at her, hatred evident even across the distance, and then he smirked in victory. Her hands balled into fists. The temptation to run down the driveway and haul her mother out of the taxi was bone deep. But she couldn't force her mom to leave Cory. It was something Mimi had to do on her own.

Leah turned and walked toward Tucker. "Sorry." The need to defend Mimi's actions clawed at her. "My mom isn't normally like that unless she's been drinking."

"I get it." He paused for a long moment. "Are you okay?"

Tucker's face was hidden in shadow, but the tenderness in his voice caused fresh tears to spring to her eyes. Her emotions were all over the place today. Leah hugged herself tighter. "I'm fine. It's been a long day."

"I should go and let you get some rest. You have my number, right?" Tucker paused and waited for her to nod. "Call if you need anything." He stepped closer and the motion-sensor light on her porch activated. Their gazes met. Tucker smiled, although it didn't quite reach his eyes. "We'll talk more about Kaylee tomorrow."

"Okay. Thanks. For everything."

He seemed to wrestle with something before his shoulders dropped. "I don't want to scare you, but I can't leave without saying this. Lock your doors tonight and use your security alarm."

She froze. "You think the attacker will come here?"

"Better to be safe than sorry."

A shiver raced along Leah's spine. Tucker's warning followed her

31

back inside and through her bedtime routine. She double- and triple-checked the locks on all the doors and windows before turning in. Jax and Coconut took their positions on the bed alongside her, the weight of their familiar forms comforting. They weren't guard dogs, by any means, but their keen hearing and protective nature would alert Leah to any trouble. She kept her night-light on and her cell phone close.

Dreams turned to nightmares. Something snapped her awake. Leah sat straight up in bed, a scream trapped in her throat. Her heart thundered and she blinked rapidly to clear her vision of the attacker choking her. Her bedsheets were tangled around her legs. Sweat coated her skin and moonlight still filtered through the slats in the blinds. Leah pressed a hand to her chest. "You're okay. It was just a dream."

But she wasn't okay. As the nightmare faded, Leah realized something was very wrong.

Jax and Coconut were both gone.

She placed a hand on the comforter and found the bed still warm from their bodies. Where were they? Leah normally locked the doggie door at night to prevent critters—like raccoons—from slipping inside the house. Coconut was also small enough to be carried away by a hawk, so she didn't go out unaccompanied after dark. The dogs woke her if they needed to use the restroom in the middle of the night. Somehow they'd slipped from the bed without her knowledge. The intensity of the nightmare had been consuming.

Leah slipped from the bed. Her entire body protested the movement, muscles sore from fighting off her attacker, reminding her of how close she'd come to dying. The hallway beyond her bedroom was dark. Silent. Fear gripped her. "Jax? Coconut?"

Her voice came out in a whisper. Leah scooped her cell phone from the nightstand, her fingers hovering over the keypad. Should she call 911? And tell them what? Her dogs were missing? It sounded silly, even in her own head. Leah hadn't even checked the house.

Perhaps her thrashing had forced Jax and Coconut to retreat to their doggie beds in the dining room.

Taking a deep breath to settle her nerves, Leah edged out of the bedroom. The carpet was soft under her bare feet. Her footsteps made no sound. Goosebumps broke out across her skin, and her instincts were to retreat to the safety of the bedroom, but a love for her dogs pushed her forward. If something had happened to them, Leah would never forgive herself.

More than likely, she'd be laughing at her silliness in the morning. Hadn't she mistaken Mimi for an intruder earlier?

The thoughts, rational and irrational, bounced in her head like ping-pong balls as Leah reached the end of the hallway. A floor lamp in the living room glowed like a welcome beacon. "Jax? Coconut?"

Silence. Something was very wrong. Leah kept moving, her footsteps growing quicker as she reached the dining room. The birds were nestled in their cages, sleeping, but the dogs' beds were empty. A breeze rippled across her pajama legs. Leah spun, her gaze shooting to the dog door. The plastic cover was off. It lay on the tile floor. Heart pounding, she stepped closer, trying to figure out what she was seeing.

Someone—or something—had punched a hole in the plastic door.

A dog yelped. The high-pitched cry of pain was familiar.

Coconut!

Grabbing a knife from the butcher block on the counter, and heedless of her own safety, Leah raced for the back door. She fumbled with the locks before bursting out of the house. Jax was barking somewhere. Far away. The sound carried on the wind. Leah scanned her fenced backyard, but she didn't see her dogs anywhere. Coconut gave another yelp. That'd come from the side of the house.

She bolted down the porch steps, stubbing her toe on the concrete in her haste to find her precious dogs. Leah barely felt the pain. She gripped the knife tightly in one hand. Shadows lurked in every corner of the property beyond the shallow porch light. Her feet slipped on the dew-coated grass.

Something in black shifted in the periphery of her vision. Leah tried to dodge it but wasn't fast enough. A man grabbed her. One arm clamped down on her waist, the other clapped over her mouth. She struggled and tried to scream, but it was no use.

He had her.

SIX

"Leah, it's me." Tucker whispered the words in her ear, hoping they'd cut through her panic. He hadn't wanted to frighten her, but grabbing her was the only way to stop her from going around the side of the house.

Where a killer was waiting.

Leah stilled in his arms. He dropped his hand from her mouth where he'd placed it to keep her from crying out. The moon slipped behind a cloud, hiding them from watchful eyes, but it wouldn't be long before the attacker wondered why Leah wasn't rushing forward to save her dog. "Get inside and lock the door behind you."

"Coconut." She whirled to face him. "Jax. Someone took them."

Was that a butcher knife in her hand? The woman was running heedlessly into a tangle with a dangerous criminal armed with only a knife? She was going to get herself killed. Tucker was a trained soldier, granted, but it'd been easy to sneak up and grab her. The man hunting her wouldn't have a problem doing the same. She was outmatched and ill-prepared. "I'll get the dogs. You have my word. Now get in the house and call the police."

Tucker gently pushed her toward the porch, and to his relief,

Leah complied. She hurried up the stairs and closed the door behind her. He waited until the lock snitched into place before turning his attention back to the side of the house.

He adjusted the hold on his handgun and eased through the shadows. Tucker mentally berated himself for taking too long at Logan's. His friend lived in the neighborhood. After leaving Leah's house, Tucker kept watch, worried her attacker would make a second attempt to hurt her. But when the hours crept by and nothing happened, he drove to Logan's for a bite of food and a quick shower to wash off the stench of the lake.

Thirty minutes. He'd been gone thirty minutes, but it was enough time for the attacker to make his move. Had he been aware of Tucker keeping watch? More than likely. Which meant this criminal was smart and careful. Not someone to be underestimated.

Tucker edged along the side of the house. A dog was barking somewhere frantically. It sounded like Jax, but the animal was too far away to be seen. From the sound of it, he was somewhere in the woods behind the house.

Movement rustled the grass. Something streaked past Tucker and raced for the back porch.

Coconut.

She raced for the doggie door and disappeared. Tucker held his breath and peeked around the side of the house. The cloud covering the moon shifted, illuminating the yard. A dark shadow was moving toward the front of the house. Escaping? Or looking for another way in? Tucker couldn't be sure, but whatever was going on, that guy had to be stopped.

"Don't move!" Tucker shouted.

The man ignored his command, whirling around instead. Tucker had a brief glimpse of something flying through the air and instinct took over. He dove for cover a heartbeat before there was an explosion of light and smoke. A flashbang.

Tucker blinked rapidly, willing his eyes to adjust. Blind, his ears ringing, he was temporarily a sitting duck. He swallowed hard and kept his gun at the ready. Shapes formed as his vision cleared.

The side yard was empty.

He bolted for the front, keeping close to the building for protection. The sound of a vehicle engine firing up fueled his steps. But it was too late. He burst into the front yard in time to see two taillights flash as the attacker escaped.

Hours later, midmorning sunshine beat down on Tucker's shoulders. Birds sang in a nearby oak tree and the humid summer air was fragrant with roses. He studied the message hastily scrawled on the side of Leah's house.

You're dead.

Nathan, Tucker's friend and a former Green Beret, rocked back on his heels in the grass. His expression was grim, brows forming a deep vee on his forehead. "The attacker wrote this on the wall before luring the dogs outside?"

Tucker nodded. "There wasn't time for him to do it afterward. I believe he snuck onto the property while I was at Logan's. He scrawled the message on the wall, broke the plastic cover over the doggie door, and using meat, convinced the dogs to come outside." Tucker waved toward the woods beyond the fence. "He tied Jax up. Probably because he was worried the Lab would attack once he started hurting Coconut. Then he used the smaller dog's cries to bait Leah into coming outside."

"That's an awful lot of trouble to go to. Why not just break into the house?"

"He's a big guy. Same size as me, roughly. I can't wiggle my shoulders through the dog door and the locks are too high to reach by sticking my arm inside. My assumption is the attacker had the same issues." Tucker frowned. "He could've taken out a window, but Leah

37

has a basic security system that covers them. The alarm would've sounded, and the company is automatically called. Luring her outside was the only way to attack her."

Nathan's gaze swept over the message again. "Is that blood?"

"Yes. Pig, according to the lab tech." Tucker's hands twitched, and he had the urge to ball them into fists. "The attacker at the lake was wearing a pig mask. He's sticking with a theme."

"Creep," Nathan muttered, anger fueling his words.

His sentiment matched Tucker's own. The reaction wasn't surprising. Nathan was fiercely loyal and protective of the people close to him. That included Leah. She and Cassie, Nathan's wife, were best friends. They'd grown up together. Along with William and Kaylee. It was a strange twist of fate that Tucker had been befriended by a man connected to his fallen comrade. His father would've said it was God at work. William, too, come to think of it.

Tucker shoved his hands in his pockets. "Leah believes these attacks are connected to her search for Kaylee. The police disagree. Chief Garcia with the Knoxville Police Department suspects Leah has picked up a stalker. Detective Walsh from the sheriff's department came by earlier this morning. He echoed the theory."

The two agencies worked independently. The Knoxville Police Department, headed by Chief Garcia, handled any crime occurring within the city while the Medina County Sheriff's Department had jurisdiction over the county. Kaylee's disappearance was being investigated by the sheriff's department, as was the attack on Leah from the lake. However, her home resided within Knoxville city limits, so the police department had responded first. Detective Walsh would lead the investigation, since the two attacks were linked, and promised to keep Chief Garcia advised.

It wasn't ideal. Tucker would've preferred Chief Garcia to be in charge. He'd worked with the man several times and found the chief to be kind, thorough, and dedicated.

"It's possible Leah has a stalker." Nathan's voice was flat, belying the turmoil bubbling under the surface of his placid exterior. It was palpable. These incidents were reminiscent of the stalker who'd terrorized Cassie. The man had been caught and was currently in a maximum security prison, but Nathan's wife had nearly lost her life in the process. Nathan blew out a breath. "But I don't think it's likely, given the circumstances."

Tucker didn't either. He gestured to the message on the wall. "Whoever this guy is, he waited until I left to make his move. This creep is smart. Careful. It makes him extremely dangerous."

"Agreed. Let's go inside and talk to Leah and Cassie."

They trudged across the yard and into the kitchen. Jax and Coconut greeted them with soft barks and a few licks. Both dogs had been examined by an emergency vet clinic. The meat the attacker fed them wasn't laced with poison, and while Coconut had a few minor sore spots, she was otherwise unharmed. A fact Tucker was grateful for. Leah loved her animals dearly, and it would've devastated her to lose them.

The two women were seated at the kitchen table. Breakfast pastries from a local bakery sat untouched between them, and the enticing scent of coffee swirled in the air. Tucker's gaze met Leah's. His heart skipped several beats. She'd pulled her curls back into a low ponytail, but a few errant strands had wriggled free to curve around her face. Bruises marked several places on her porcelain skin.

Something about the woman tugged at his protective instincts. Yes, she was stunningly beautiful, but it was far more than that. There was a vulnerability and a sweetness to her, but underneath was the soul of a warrior. Last night, she ran out of the house to protect what she loved. He admired that. Tucker also respected her push to find answers about Kaylee's disappearance.

"What do you think?" Cassie asked.

Nathan crossed the room and placed a hand on his wife's shoulder before reaching down and picking up her cup of coffee. "Well, two attacks within the span of a few hours isn't good." He cast

39

Leah a sympathetic look. "I don't think you should go anywhere by yourself for the time being."

She sagged against her chair. "I suspected that's what you would say."

"Don't worry about the shelter," Cassie said quickly. "I'll pick up your shifts, or one of the other employees can cover them. The paperwork and finances can be done remotely."

Tucker crossed the room and selected a mug from the peg next to the coffee machine. He poured himself a generous serving of the dark brew. His eyes were gritty from spending most of the night keeping watch over Leah's house. Not that it had stopped anything. She'd still been attacked. "We should arrange for the guys to guard the house. Chief Garcia is going to increase patrols, but I don't think that's enough of a deterrent."

Their friend group consisted of veterans, trained soldiers who wouldn't hesitate to put their lives on the line to protect innocent people. They'd banded together to guard women in danger before. Three members of their group—Jason, Nathan, and Kyle—had fallen in love during the dangerous situations. That wouldn't happen with Tucker. Marriage wasn't anywhere on his radar.

Nathan shared a glance with Tucker. "I agree. Leah needs protection until this criminal is caught. I'll talk to the others and we'll make arrangements."

"Hold on." Leah jutted up her chin. "I understand the need for precautions, but I'm not hiding out in my home until this guy is caught. These attacks are linked to my search for Kaylee, which means I'm getting close to something. I have to keep going."

Tucker stiffened. "That's a bad idea—"

"I already know what you're going to say." Leah held up a hand, her gaze darting between Nathan and Tucker. "Leave the investigation to you guys. But I can't do that. I started this and I have to see it through."

Tucker wanted to argue with her, but from the stubborn tilt to

Leah's chin, there wasn't a way to dissuade her. There was only one viable option. Leah needed a full-time bodyguard. "I'll help you search for Kaylee. We can do it together."

Leah was quiet for a long moment. "Why, Tucker? Why do you want to help me?"

"Because William saved my life. He took the bullet that was meant for me. I tried to save him but..." He couldn't. Tucker swallowed the lump clogging his throat and forced himself to meet Leah's gaze. Her complexion was pale, mouth slightly parted. In shock? Probably. Nathan and Cassie's expressions were similar. Tucker had never spoken about William's death or his reason for coming to Knoxville. Some things were too painful for words. "Before he died, William asked me to deliver his personal items to his sister, but when I arrived in town, she was already missing. I believed the police when they claimed Kaylee ran off. But these recent attacks change things. If there's something I can do to help her, then I have to try."

Tucker had made so many mistakes in his life. Had so many regrets. This couldn't be one of them. He wouldn't allow it. "I owe it to William. And Kaylee. Let me help you, Leah. Together we can do this."

SEVEN

Leah waved goodbye as Nathan and Cassie backed out of the driveway. They'd spent the last thirty minutes developing a game plan to keep her safe. Tucker would stay close, helping to work Kaylee's case, while other members of their friend group took turns guarding the house at night. Additionally, Nathan would also keep a close eye on Cassie. The attacker had proven he was capable and determined. It wasn't a stretch to imagine he'd use people Leah cared about against her. It was terrifying to think about, but Nathan would keep her best friend safe. He'd die before letting anyone hurt her.

Leah's attention skated to the former Army Ranger leaning against the porch pillar. Tucker's posture was casual, but his gaze scanned their surroundings. Children across the street yelped with joyous cries as they jumped through a sprinkler. Mrs. Bowman was weeding her flowerbeds, a giant hat shading her face. Two older women were enjoying a glass of ice tea on rocking chairs at the Fredrick house. Normal everyday life.

Leah wrapped her arms around herself. "I love this neighborhood. It's hard to believe a criminal slipped through my fence, wrote a message in pig's blood on my house, and terrorized my dogs."

Tucker was quiet for a long moment. "You don't have to look for Kaylee yourself, Leah. I meant what I said. I'll see this through."

She shook her head, resolve straightening her spine. "No. Whoever is behind this wants to scare me into submission. That's not going to happen." Leah had survived surgery, fifteen rounds of intensive chemo, and permanent scarring. "I'm tougher than I look. Cancer couldn't take me down. This monster won't either."

"Cancer?"

Heat colored Leah's cheeks. She'd forgotten for a moment that Tucker didn't know. Why did telling him matter? She couldn't say, except that for some inexplicable reason, it did. Maybe because of this attraction humming between them. Or at least, from her side. Tucker had never given any indication that he saw her as anything more than Cassie's good friend. But if Leah was being honest with herself, she wanted Tucker to look at her. To really see her.

As a woman. As desirable.

Finding out she had cancer, and all the messiness that went with it, was a surefire way to douse any spark of attraction on his part. She was damaged goods. Horrible to say and think, but there was no getting around it. Men could carry scars and be considered handsome or rugged. For women...it was disfigurement.

Leah swallowed hard, focusing her attention on an errant leaf on her porch. "I was diagnosed with a rare form of breast cancer shortly after graduating from college. I'm in remission now, but it was a long road to get here."

Was she still in remission? The test results hadn't come in yet. This final year was a milestone. If the cancer didn't return within five years, the chances of having it return were slim. It was something Leah didn't want to think about right now. She couldn't control or change it. Some things were strictly in God's hands.

Tucker's boots thumped against the wooden planks of the porch. He joined Leah at the railing, standing close enough for their shoulders to touch. "My dad had cancer." Tucker's voice was hollow with pain. "Lung. Irony was, he never smoked a day in his life. I was overseas when he died, but my aunt said he fought hard to beat it." He glanced at her then. "I'm glad you did."

Leah's breath hitched. The emotions shimmering in the depths of his emerald eyes made her heart quicken. Illogical and unreasonable. But it was a reaction she couldn't control. This man had saved her life twice, and now he was looking at her with such admiration and respect. It was a heady feeling. One Leah liked far more than she should. "I'm sorry about your dad. Losing him must've been hard."

"It was. We'd always been incredibly close, but he didn't tell me about the cancer diagnosis. Pop didn't want me to cut my military career short. I found out after he passed away."

Leah couldn't imagine how difficult that must've been for Tucker. She searched for the right words to console him, but before she could, he cleared his throat. "We should talk about Kaylee."

"Right." Leah sensed Tucker was uneasy with the direction of their conversation. It was understandable. They'd trod into some personal matters. She was feeling vulnerable herself. Leah backed away from the railing. "Let's go inside. I could use more coffee."

Fifteen minutes later, they each had a fresh cup of coffee and a pastry in front of them. The uneasiness of their interaction on the porch had melted away as quickly as fog disappearing in the sunshine. Leah joined Tucker at the table. "How much do you know about Kaylee's disappearance?"

"Only what the police told me. It's an active investigation, so they didn't share much. She was last seen closing up the vet clinic where she worked. No one has heard from her since."

Leah took a long sip of her coffee. "Kaylee had an apartment near her work. It was her habit to walk home after locking up the vet clinic. The night she disappeared, it was raining. Heavily. I believe Kaylee accepted a ride from someone—someone she knew and trusted—and her faith in that person turned out to be a mistake."

"The police didn't consider that?"

"Detective Walsh believes Kaylee ran away with her boyfriend. To my knowledge, he's never considered any other theory." Leah's hand tightened around her mug. It wouldn't be easy to tell Tucker this, but he needed to understand why Detective Walsh's judgment was clouded. "Let me back up a bit. When her brother was deployed the first time, Kaylee struggled. She and William were incredibly close—being twins made that bond even stronger—and I think the knowledge that he was in danger every single day ate her up. She started using drugs to cope."

Tucker winced. "What kind?"

"Prescription meds mostly. Kaylee mixed them with alcohol, which made things worse. I knew something was wrong, but she refused to talk about it. Eventually, while driving under the influence, Kaylee slammed her car into a light pole. Nearly killed herself. It was a wake-up call. The judge offered her the option to attend rehab instead of jail time, and Kaylee took the lifeline. She did 90 days inpatient, came home, and started attending Narcotics Anonymous meetings. She took her sobriety seriously." Leah pushed her coffee away. "Unfortunately, her actions were enough to label her as a troublemaker and a drug user. It didn't help that Kaylee's father also abused drugs. He died of an overdose when she and William were fifteen. Detective Walsh has known her family for a long time. He arrested her father on numerous occasions as a patrol officer."

"You think he's biased?"

She nodded. "After Kaylee disappeared, there was a rumor going around town that she had a secret boyfriend. Walsh believes this guy was probably bad news, which is why Kaylee didn't tell any of her friends about him. Maybe a drug user. That's why Kaylee disappeared and hasn't contacted anyone. She doesn't want us to know where she is or what she's doing."

Tucker wiped his mouth and beard with a napkin and then tossed it on his empty plate. "Let me play devil's advocate for a moment. Isn't it possible that's exactly what happened?"

"No. Like I said before, Kaylee took her sobriety very seriously." Leah jabbed her finger on the table for emphasis. "She attended an NA meeting the day before her disappearance, and her sponsor says she was staying clean. Not to mention, the rumor about Kaylee's secret boyfriend began circulating Knoxville *after* she disappeared. It could've been started by anyone. Including the person who took her. I never put much stock in it." She tried to keep the irritation out of her voice, but it was hard. Leah was tired of people not listening to her. "I know Kaylee. Something is wrong. These attacks on me prove it. Renting the billboard and offering a reward for information on Kaylee's case made me a target."

His expression darkened. "Someone doesn't want you putting pressure on the police to find Kaylee. Or is scared you'll receive a tip that'll point you in the right direction."

"Yes."

Tucker leaned back in his chair. The silence stretched out between them and Leah let it. Her head was pounding, her neck sore, and her patience razor-thin. She didn't want to be in the center of this tornado, but there was no way to avoid it. Giving up would mean accepting that Kaylee might never be found. That wasn't an option Leah could live with.

Jax nudged Tucker's elbow with his snout. The dogs liked him. It meant something to Leah. She'd learned over the years that animals were a great judge of character. Coconut pawed at Leah's leg and she lifted the little dog into her lap. The move was rewarded with several puppy kisses on her chin.

Tucker complied with Jax's silent request, gently rubbing the Lab's ears, seemingly deep in thought. Finally, he sighed. "Given everything you've said, I agree. The timing of the attacks on you so soon after the billboard went up feels like too much of a coincidence. And Kaylee's disappearance needs to be looked into further. Can you think of anyone who'd want to hurt her?"

Some of the tension eased from Leah's spine. It was one thing to have Tucker alongside her as a bodyguard while she investigated. Quite another for him to believe her. Leah hadn't realized how much she'd wanted the latter until now. She stroked Coconut's silky fur. "It's hard for me to imagine anyone I know is a kidnapper, but there is someone I've suspected for a while. Holt Adler, the town vet. He was Kaylee's boss."

Tucker's brows winged up. "The same Holt Adler that threatened Cassie not too long ago?"

"Yep." Leah's best friend had been stalked, and while Holt hadn't turned out to be the culprit, he'd been a suspect. "Kaylee mentioned Holt had asked her out a few times, but she felt uncomfortable dating her boss. She turned him down. I've wondered for a while if he took it more personally than she realized. I'd like to go to the vet's office this morning and talk to him. We can take Jax and Coconut. Use them as a cover. I'm sure word has spread through Knoxville about the attack last night. It would make sense to have Coconut and Jax checked for injuries. There's no way for Holt to know we took them to the emergency vet last night."

"That sounds like a good plan to me." Tucker paused, and then his gaze lifted to Leah's. "One thing before we go. You're smart, so I'm sure you've already thought of this, but I have to say it anyway. This may not have the ending you're hoping for."

Leah's gut clenched. "Because Kaylee may be dead." She didn't wait for him to respond, but continued, "I know. I'm aware. And now that we've had this conversation, I need to ask something of you. We continue on as though Kaylee is alive. No matter what. Until we know for certain that she's gone..."

There was always hope. It's what got Leah through cancer, and it would see her through this as well. Prayers and hope.

Please, God, give me the strength and wisdom to find her.

EIGHT

Knoxville Veterinarian Clinic was on the outskirts of town, close to the freeway. Tucker glanced in the sideview mirror as Leah pulled into the generous parking lot. No one had followed them, but he wouldn't let his guard down for a moment. Two separate attacks had been made in the last twenty-four hours. The assailant was determined to kill Leah, and he wouldn't stop until he'd succeeded or was in prison.

"That's the billboard." Leah pointed to a large sign, visible above the tall pine trees. A black-and-white photograph of Kaylee took up one side. Blonde hair tumbled to her shoulders, a bright smile on her face. She looked young and vibrant. Alongside Kaylee's photograph was information about her disappearance, a request for information, the promise of a reward, and a phone number to call. The billboard was angled so travelers would see it on their way out of town and from the nearby freeway.

"Have you received any phone calls to the tip line?" Tucker asked.

"Not yet, but the sign went up last week." Leah killed the engine and grabbed her purse. "The number goes to an answering service who takes a message and then passes it on to me. I plan on giving everything to Detective Walsh." Her nose wrinkled. "Not that I think he'll do anything with it."

Tucker couldn't argue with that sentiment. He hadn't been impressed with Detective Walsh either. "After I arrived in town and found out Kaylee had left, I tried to locate extended family members but couldn't."

"They didn't have anyone other than each other." Leah's voice was sad. "Their mom was killed in a car accident a few years after their dad died. Kaylee and William lived with their grandmother after that, but she passed away two years ago."

A pang of sympathy struck his heart. "No wonder Kaylee struggled after William was deployed." Turning to drugs wasn't the answer, but sometimes people made mistakes when dealing with complicated emotions. "William constantly worried about her while we were overseas. He wrote Kaylee every chance he had. He was talking about getting out of the military..."

Instead of coming home, William had been shot dead. The image of his friend's face flashed in Tucker's mind. Skin coated with dust, eyes pleading. *Promise you'll take care of Kaylee.*

"Tucker." Leah's hand brushed across his forearm, jolting him out of the memory. "Are you okay? You're a thousand miles away."

"I'm okay." Except he wasn't. Not even close. And Tucker secretly feared he would never be again. Nine months hadn't been enough to take the edge off his grief or wipe away the nightmares plaguing him. Layered over that was guilt. He should've looked for Kaylee sooner instead of relying on the police assessment, but now wasn't the time to make a list of his failures or tackle his issues. There was a mission to complete. Tucker needed to keep Leah safe and find Kaylee.

He turned back to the matter at hand. "How far away was Kaylee's apartment from here?"

Leah pointed to the right. "She lived three blocks that way. After she disappeared, I put her stuff into storage. It's still there."

She was incredible. Tucker couldn't think of any childhood friends that would've done the same for him if he'd gone missing. Now, things were different. Nathan and the rest of their group would storm the countryside looking for him, but their bond was unusual, in his opinion. "You're a good friend, Leah."

The compliment seemed to surprise her. Behind the frames of her glasses, her gorgeous eyes widened before a crease settled between her brows. "Do you think so? Too often, it feels like I've completely failed Kaylee." She shoved a curly lock behind her ear. "Keeping her stuff in storage is a poor substitute for finding her."

"Don't be so hard on yourself. You're not a police officer. From where I'm sitting, you've done everything in your power to bring her home."

Their gazes caught and held. Tucker was mesmerized by the color of her eyes. They were chocolate-brown with flecks of golden highlights. The curls framing her exquisite face were soft and loose. One curved along her forehead, and for a heartbeat, Tucker was tempted to brush it back. He resisted. Romance would only complicate matters between them, and things were already complex enough. Not to mention he wasn't the marrying type. And Leah...well, Leah deserved forever.

A yip came from the rear of the SUV, breaking the moment. Leah smiled and released her seat belt. "Okay, Coconut. I hear you."

"Hold on. Let me come around." Tucker hopped out of the vehicle. He settled a baseball cap on his head to shade his vision from the bright sunlight before scanning the parking lot and surrounding area. A woman exited the vet clinic with a cat carrier in her hand. She barely glanced at him as she hurried to her vehicle. Obviously not a threat. Tucker opened Leah's door. "We're good."

She exited the SUV and clicked the fob. The rear hatch of the vehicle slowly opened, revealing Coconut in a small dog carrier and

Jax belted in place for safety with a special leash. He whimpered, casting a forlorn look at the vet clinic.

Leah reached for the Lab. "I'll take Jax. He's a sweetie most of the time, but the clinic makes him nervous. They have to put a muzzle on him for examinations. Can you handle Coconut?"

"Sure thing." Tucker popped open the cage and then snapped a leash on the Chihuahua. He lifted her into his arms. She licked the underside of his chin. A warmth spread through his chest as he rubbed her ears in response. He'd never been much of a pet person, but Leah's dogs were converting him with every passing minute.

The hair on the back of Tucker's neck stood up. He glanced over his shoulder but saw nothing unusual. Still, the feeling of being watched crept over him. His gaze shot to the clinic, and movement in the window caught his attention. A reflection in the glass? Or had someone inside been watching them?

Uneasiness settled in his gut. For the dozenth time, Tucker second-guessed their plan. But what other choice was there? Leah was determined to find Kaylee, and if he was being honest, Tucker deeply admired her commitment. Convincing her to take a step back had failed. The next best thing was keeping a sharp eye for any attacks.

A blast of cold air greeted Tucker as he followed Leah into the clinic. It was a welcome relief from the humid heat. The visitor chairs in the reception area were empty. Tucker half-listened as Leah greeted the woman behind the front desk. The door leading to an exam room opened.

Holt Alder appeared. Mid-thirties, roughly 6 feet tall and 190 pounds, with a confident walk that bordered on a swagger. He was dressed in navy surgical scrubs and a white lab coat. His tennis shoes were designer. A small tear cut across the left one near the toe.

Tucker had never interacted with him, but when Nathan's wife, Cassie, was being stalked, Holt was one of their top suspects. His background check hadn't yielded anything alarming, but Tucker made a mental note to do another one. Just in case. Holt's body style and height were similar to Leah's attacker, but something felt off. He couldn't place what though.

Holt stopped at the counter, offering a sympathetic smile. "It's good to see you, Leah. I figured you'd be coming in today with the dogs. Half a dozen people told me about the attack last night." His gaze swept over her. "Are you okay?"

Jax growled, the hair on the back of his neck rising. Tucker couldn't blame the mutt. He was feeling the same way. The intensity of Holt's stare was off-putting. Even Coconut snuggled closer into Tucker's embrace.

Leah patted Jax's head. "I'm okay, Holt. Thanks for asking." She gestured toward Tucker. "This is my friend, Tucker Colburn."

Holt nodded in his direction. "Nice to meet you."

"Likewise."

Jax growled again and Holt retrieved a muzzle from the counter. He handed it to Leah. "I'll let you do the honors." Holt smiled, but it didn't reach his eyes. "One of these days, I'm going to convince Jax to like me."

"Don't take it personally," Leah said. "He does it with every vet."

That was true. When they'd gone to the emergency vet last night, Jax had acted the same way. Leah slipped the muzzle over Jax's snout with a lot of loving words and a kiss to the forehead. Then Holt led them to an exam room. He quickly but thoroughly gave the pups a once-over, declaring them to be in perfect health.

"You were lucky, Leah." Holt removed his plastic gloves and dumped them in a nearby trash can. "Whoever attacked you could have fed them poisoned meat. My receptionist mentioned that you'd been attacked earlier the same day on the lake. What on earth is going on?"

Leah quickly gave a rundown of both incidents. "I believe these attacks are connected to my search for Kaylee."

Holt whistled, concern darkening his eyes. He leaned against the counter and crossed his arms. "I never liked the way Detective Walsh handled her case, but to come after you doesn't make sense. It brings more attention to Kaylee's disappearance. It would seem whoever was behind this would want the exact opposite."

She shrugged. "Depends on whether the police believe the cases are linked. Right now, they don't." Her hand tightened on Jax's leash. "Did anything unusual happen the day Kaylee disappeared?"

"No. It was a regular day. She came into work around noon, handled all the patients, and locked up. I was called out to the Granger farm to assist one of their mares. She had a breached birth, and they were worried." Holt heaved a sigh. "It stormed something fierce that night. There were tornado warnings in effect. I called the office to offer Kaylee a ride home, but she'd already left."

"Were you far when you called her?" Tucker asked.

"I hadn't left the Granger farm yet. Kaylee would've had to wait about thirty minutes, but I figured it was better than walking home in the storm." He shook his head. "I wish she'd been here..."

His shoulders sagged. Holt's sadness appeared genuine, but that could be faked. His whereabouts, however, were easy to confirm by checking with the Grangers. If Holt was telling the truth, he had an alibi for the time Kaylee disappeared.

From the expression on Leah's face, she'd figured out the same thing. "Can you think of anyone who might want to hurt Kaylee?"

Holt opened his mouth and then closed it again. Then he sighed. "I've told Detective Walsh everything I know, and I don't want to point fingers at innocent people. It's best if you leave the investigation to the police, Leah. Seems you're in enough danger as it is."

"All I want is the truth. Please, Holt."

Her pleading tone had no effect on the other man. Holt barely glanced at her as he opened the exam room door. "Sorry. I've said all I'm going to about the matter. Y'all stay safe."

Tucker had to fight the urge to give Holt a piece of his mind. How could he keep vital information about Kaylee's disappearance quiet? Especially with Leah in danger? Then again, he'd told the police. Tucker's real problem was with Detective Walsh, not Holt.

He waited while Leah paid the bill, and then they exited the clinic. Her disappointment was palpable. She glanced over her shoulder as they crossed the parking lot. "What do you think?"

"Holt knows more than he's saying, but I don't think he's involved in Kaylee's disappearance. He had an alibi for that night. I'll ask Nathan to speak to the Grangers, but it doesn't make sense for Holt to lie about something we could easily verify."

"I'm not so sure about that. This is the first time Holt mentioned being at the Grangers' farm on the night Kaylee went missing. It's been nine months and memories can be a funny thing. The Grangers will probably vouch that Holt was there, but they may not remember what time he left."

Tucker mulled over her observation. "He's covering his tracks."

"Maybe. I don't think we should take him off the suspect list yet." Leah blew out a breath as she lifted the rear hatch on her SUV. Jax, free of the muzzle and happy to be out of the vet's office, jumped straight into the vehicle.

The roar of an engine caught Tucker's attention. He spun toward the parking lot entrance just as a massive pickup truck swung in. Leah inhaled sharply. "Oh, no. It's Cory."

"Cory, your stepfather?"

Leah nodded. Tucker quickly shoved Coconut into the carrier and shut the door. He needed his hands free. Something in Leah's voice, along with Cory's driving, put him on edge.

There was about to be a confrontation.

NINE

Cory was madder than a hornet.

Dread pooled in Leah's stomach as her stepfather exited his oversized truck. His olive green T-shirt bore sweat stains and his camouflage pants matched the hat pulled low on his forehead. The expression etched on his features was stormy as he marched across the parking lot.

Leah forced herself to straighten her shoulders and meet his heated glare. Cory was a bully, plain and simple. They'd never gotten along, although she attempted to keep the peace for her mother's sake. It was a complicated and delicate dance. One Leah despised.

"You sent the police to my house," Cory spat. His voice carried across the distance between them. His ears were red with rage. "How dare you tell people lies about me."

Cory's hands balled into fists. Beside her, Tucker stiffened. Leah placed a hand on his arm to prevent him from stepping forward to intercede. Her stepfather wouldn't hit her. No, he was smarter than that. Whatever anger he had toward Leah would be directed at her mom.

That thought sent another crippling wave of dread to cramp her stomach. Leah wanted to double over from the pain. She couldn't bear the idea of her mother being hurt. Especially by a man who was supposed to love and cherish her. Leah had tried so many times to convince Mimi to leave Cory, but her mom refused. Abuse was an insidious thing.

"I didn't send the police to your house." Her tone was calm, belying the emotions rumbling below the surface. Leah still had her hand on Tucker's arm. His muscles were rock hard under her palm, his gaze locked on Cory, his jaw tight as if he was grinding his teeth together. He looked positively dangerous. Lethal. Controlled. It was a glimpse of the Army Ranger he'd been.

The intensity of his protection should've scared her, but it didn't. Tucker's reaction was calculated and measured. Respectful. He hadn't moved an inch since she'd placed her hand on his arm, nor had he shaken off her touch. He would safeguard Leah with his life. It made her feel safe for the first time in a very long time. Maybe the first time ever.

Cory must've also sensed Tucker's willingness to protect Leah, because he stopped several paces away from them. He glared. "Oh yeah? Then explain to me why Chief Garcia was at my house this morning, asking all kinds of questions about where I was last night." Cory's scowl deepened. "I don't appreciate being accused of something I didn't do."

Leah's heart skipped a beat. For the first time, she noticed her stepfather's height and weight. He was about the size of the man who'd chased her at the lake. Cory had always kept in good shape. There also wasn't any love lost between them. Could he be responsible for the attacks against her?

Her mouth suddenly went dry. Leah swallowed hard. "Chief Garcia is working with the sheriff's department to figure out who is behind the attacks against me. I'm sure he didn't mean to accuse you of anything."

Cory ignored her comment and jabbed a motor-oil-stained finger in her direction. "Keep my name out of your mouth, understand me? I don't take kindly to people interfering in my life."

"That sounds dangerously close to a threat."

Tucker's voice was low, but the quiet anger buried in his words warned he was being pushed to action. From the rear of the SUV, Jax growled and bared his teeth. He strained against the leash holding him inside the vehicle. Any other time, Leah might've admired the way her dog was so in tune with Tucker, but this situation was far too precarious.

Not one to back down, Cory puffed out his chest and shot Tucker a look of derision. "You stay out of it. This is family business."

Sensing an escalation in the situation, Leah stepped between the two men. "I'm sorry Chief Garcia came to question you. I'll talk to him."

The apology was ridiculous, but she didn't have any pride when it came to protecting her mom. Cory had used his fists more than once. Leah couldn't stop herself from trying to diffuse his temper.

"Make sure you do." Cory's gaze hardened. "Don't make me mad, Leah. You'll regret it."

With those parting words, he spun on his heel and marched back to his truck. The engine revved and then he peeled out of the parking lot.

Leah let go of the breath she was holding and sagged against her SUV's tailgate. Jax, sensing her emotional state, snuggled up next to her. It was at least ninety degrees, but an icy chill had settled in her bones. She wrapped her arms around her dog.

Tucker fired up the SUV, turning the air-conditioning on high before returning to the rear hatch. He pushed Coconut's cage farther into the SUV and sat down next to Leah. "Are you okay?"

She could lie, but what was the point? Leah sighed. "No. As you can probably tell, Cory isn't a nice guy. He abuses my mom. Maintaining a relationship with her while she's married to him has been difficult."

"That's why you apologized."

She stroked Jax, letting his silky fur slip through her fingers. "Yes. Cory won't take out his anger on me, but he will on my mom. I've tried to convince her to leave him several times, but she won't. Healthy boundaries aren't in her wheelhouse. She's struggled with self-esteem issues for a long time." Leah didn't enjoy discussing this, but she and Tucker would spend a lot of time together in the next few days. He'd likely have more interactions with her family. "My mom got pregnant with me when she was only sixteen. Her parents were angry and insisted she marry my dad. It didn't last. He left Knoxville a year later."

"Do you have any contact with him?"

"Some." She shrugged. "He lives in Colorado with his wife and their kids. He sends me an email every now and again, but we aren't close. My mom is the one who raised me."

Tucker's gaze drifted across the parking lot. "I know what that's like. My mom left when I was ten. We don't have much contact either. Dad was the one who raised me. It does something, you know? When it's just the two of you."

Some knot of tension uncoiled inside Leah. He got it. The intricacies of a complicated relationship, the push-pull that developed over years of relying on each other. Few people did. Tucker kept surprising her. Underneath all the armor designed to keep people at arm's length was a deep thinker. Leah tilted her head. "I misjudged you."

He started, his gaze swinging toward hers. "What do you mean?"

"You're quiet and give off this don't-bother-me air. Honestly, I thought you didn't like me." She wrinkled her nose. "I had the impression you considered me vapid."

"No one who spends five minutes in your presence would think that. You're amazing, Leah." Tucker fiddled with the A/C vent, aiming the blast of cold air into Coconut's crate. "I'm sorry if I made you feel bad. It has nothing to do with you. I'm difficult to get to know. Talking about my feelings and my past isn't something I'm good at."

Another thing they had in common. Leah swept her own feelings under the rug and ignored them, but that only worked for so long. At some point, the mound was too big to step over. "I struggled with the same thing. William was the one who taught me the importance of sharing my burdens."

That brought a smile to Tucker's face. "He had a way, didn't he? Of slipping past all the noise to find the heart of the issue." The joy melted from his face. "I miss him."

"I do too."

Leah reached out and took Tucker's hand. The move was meant to be comforting, but when he flipped his palm over and interlocked their fingers, tendrils of warmth climbed up her arm. He rubbed a thumb over the ridge of her knuckle. Her heart skipped several beats. She swallowed hard, battling back the attraction flaring to the surface. It wouldn't be smart to become romantically involved with Tucker. Not while they were searching for Kaylee.

She gently pulled away under the guise of adjusting Jax's leash. "We should get these guys home."

"Absolutely." Tucker stood. He cocked his head, his attention drawn to the billboard visible over the pine trees. "Do you think it's possible Cory is involved in Kaylee's disappearance?"

Leah frowned. "I doubt it. Kaylee wouldn't have accepted a ride from him."

Tucker arched his brows. "You're assuming she got into the car willingly. We don't have proof of that. Kaylee could've been ambushed and forced into the vehicle."

He was right. A niggle of doubt tugged at her. Cory's aggression had been extreme, even for him. Could he be involved somehow? It wasn't something she'd even considered before now. "Cory has a record of violence. Mostly bar fights and domestic abuse allegations. He doesn't strike me as the kind to plan an abduction." Her fingers tightened around her keys. "But he is smart. Cory has spent a handful of days in county lockup, no more. He knows how to wriggle out of trouble."

"Which means we shouldn't underestimate him."

"No." Leah bit her lip. "Let's go talk to Kaylee's sponsor, Megan. She may have some insight that'll help."

Twenty-five minutes later, they'd dropped off the dogs at Leah's house and arranged to meet Kaylee's sponsor, Megan Ingles, at the local coffee shop.

Roasted Beans was on Main Street. The bright yellow awning was cheery, and the sign posted outside the establishment boasted a cinnamon roll and iced coffee bargain. Leah's stomach growled. She hadn't eaten much for breakfast. "I'm getting the special."

"That sounds good. I'll get the same."

Tucker held the door open for her. The scent of coffee and vanilla tickled her senses. Megan waved from a corner table in the rear. Her blonde hair was cut in a face-framing bob and she was dressed casually in a flowered top and blue jeans. A cross hung from around her neck.

Megan was a certified therapist. She ran the local NA meetings held at the church in addition to her private practice. She'd struggled with addiction in college after a car accident some twenty years ago and dedicated her life to helping others stay sober.

Leah waved back before placing their order at the counter. Tucker insisted on paying. Old-fashioned manners were as much a part of him as his military service. He even placed a hand on the small of Leah's back, gently steering her through the coffee shop to the table. She wasn't one to swoon or get giddy over a man, but Tucker was testing every one of her preconceived notions. The heat from his touch seemed to sear her skin.

Megan rose from her chair and greeted Leah with a hug. "I heard about the attacks through the grapevine. I'm so glad you're okay."

"Thanks, Megan." She hugged her friend back and then introduced Tucker. The next few minutes were a flurry of activity as the waitress brought their order. Leah tore into the soft cinnamon roll and popped a piece in her mouth. A mix of flavors burst on her tongue. "Oh, that's good." She pushed the plate toward Megan. "Would you like some?"

"If you insist." Megan grinned and broke off a piece of the roll. Then her expression grew serious. "I'm glad you called me, Leah. Rumors are flying around town, and the leading theory is that these attacks are connected to Kaylee's disappearance. How much of that is true?"

"It's a strong possibility." Leah explained her theory but didn't include her suspicions about Holt or Cory. She didn't want to bias Megan against either man. "The police are convinced Kaylee ran off, but I don't believe it. Someone doesn't want me looking into this case. Can you think of anyone who might want to hurt her?"

Megan hesitated, and then she let out a long sigh. "There's something you should know."

TEN

Tucker forgot all about his cinnamon roll and iced coffee. The urge to lean in and question Megan was strong, but he resisted. It was better for Leah to take the lead since she had a friendship with the other woman.

Megan ran a hand through her hair, ruffling the blonde strands. The bracelets on her arm jingled. "A few weeks before her disappearance, Kaylee went to Chief Garcia and reported what she knew about the drugs circulating Knoxville. It's been a problem for a while —mostly pills, like Oxycodone and meth—but the authorities haven't been able to narrow down the source." She lifted her gaze, and the look in her eyes was haunted. "Kaylee claimed Cory was her dealer."

Leah inhaled sharply. "What?"

Her complexion went pale, and she trembled. Tucker placed a hand over hers, hoping to provide some measure of comfort. Was this the information Holt had alluded to in his office? It was possible. Tucker could understand why he might hesitate to tell Leah. Cory was her stepfather and the relationship between them complicated.

Megan licked her lips. "Maybe I should've told you sooner but...I personally spoke with Detective Walsh and Chief Garcia about my concerns right after Kaylee went missing. They both promised me they'd look into the matter."

It seemed Chief Garcia had. He'd questioned Cory this morning about the attack on Leah, since the two cases could be connected. The drug trade was lucrative even in small towns. Cory had a lot to lose if he was caught.

Leah sat stone-still. In shock? Tucker couldn't blame her. He kept ahold of her hand, but his attention was locked on Megan. She looked devastated. "When did Kaylee share the information she had on Cory with Chief Garcia?"

"About two weeks before her disappearance."

A flush crept up Leah's neck. "How could you keep this a secret from me?"

"Kaylee was worried about how this news would affect you. She made me promise not to tell." Megan's eyes were pleading. "I'm sorry. I thought keeping her secret was the right thing to do. I never intended for you to be hurt."

Leah pressed her fingers to her eyelids. Her dark hair fell like a curtain covering her face, and she was silent for a long minute. Then she took a deep breath. "I'm sorry, Megs. I'm not mad at you. I just... I'm shocked. I wish I'd known this earlier."

"I think we should talk to Chief Garcia," Tucker suggested gently. "He may have an update on the case. There's a chance Cory isn't responsible for this."

Leah dropped her hand. "I'm not sure which outcome I'm hoping for. Cory isn't a nice guy—there's no question about that—but a drug dealer? It'd be impossible to keep something like that from my mom."

"Don't jump ahead. Cory doesn't strike me as the type to go home and explain what he's been doing all day. Your mom could be completely in the dark. Let's take things one step at a time." Tucker turned back to Megan. "After Kaylee went to the police, did she complain of Cory bothering her? Or did she feel like someone was watching her?"

Megan hesitated and then nodded. "Kaylee suspected someone had been inside her apartment a few times. Nothing was missing and the lock wasn't broken, but she noticed several items out of place, like someone had searched through her things. She reported it. But honestly, Kaylee was jumpy after she spoke to Chief Garcia. Cory scared her. She knew it was risky to turn him into the authorities."

"Scared her how?"

"He threatened her after she went to rehab. Nothing direct or specific, but Cory made it clear that if she went to the police about him, he'd make her pay. It took Kaylee a long time before she decided to defy him."

Leah shook her head. "I can't believe she was going through all this. I had no idea. What kind of friend does that make me?"

"A good one." Megan shoved aside the half-eaten cinnamon roll. "Please don't beat yourself up. Kaylee purposely kept this secret from you. She knew you'd worry endlessly about your mom and there wasn't anything you could do to help. I think if the police had arrested Cory or something had come from the investigation, she would've explained everything."

The more Tucker found out about Kaylee, the more he liked her. William hadn't been the only brave one in the family. Kaylee had taken a big risk to turn Cory in.

Megan glanced at her watch. "Shucks, I have to run. I have a client in fifteen minutes."

She rose from her chair. Leah and Tucker did as well. Megan embraced Leah, hugging her tight. "I'm really sorry. If you have any other questions, call me. Day or night." She pulled back. "And please, don't investigate Cory yourself. Leave it to the police. I've not had any interactions with him myself, but I've heard stories from others. He's dangerous."

"I'll be careful." Leah glanced at Tucker. "I have my own personal bodyguard, if you haven't noticed."

The warmth in her gaze sent butterflies alight in his stomach.

Tucker willed himself to get a grip. He was a grown man, not a schoolboy with a crush. But something about Leah wriggled right past all his defenses. The woman was a serious danger to his heart.

After Megan said a final goodbye and left, Leah turned to Tucker. "I think you're right. Let's go talk to Chief Garcia. I'd like to know what he thinks."

They took their iced coffees in hand and stepped into the summer heat. The police station was a block away, so despite the warm temperatures, they elected to walk.

Tucker shortened his stride to keep pace with Leah's petite stature. A light breeze ruffled her curls. The sunshine brought out the caramel highlights among the dark strands. She had a pensive look on her face. He nudged her with his elbow. "Penny for your thoughts?"

"I'm just mulling over everything Megan told me. It's a lot to take in." She breathed out a long sigh. "Kaylee was probably right to keep this from me. I would've worried obsessively about my mom."

"You love her. It's normal to want your family to be safe."

"I know, but we can't control everything. Some things we have to give to God. I've struggled with that aspect of my faith." She smiled ruefully. "In case you haven't noticed, I'm a fixer."

He chuckled. "I've noticed."

"You...you're not a believer, are you?" Leah paused and then quickly said, "Sorry. Maybe that question is out of line. I don't want to make you uncomfortable."

"No, it's okay." Tucker didn't normally talk about his faith, or lack thereof, but something about Leah made him feel reassured. As though she wouldn't judge him. "It's not that I don't believe in God. I do. But...I can't make sense of Him. I don't understand why He would allow awful things to happen."

"Like William's death?"

Her question was like a punch to his gut. Man, the woman had a way of seeing right through him. Tucker swallowed past the lump of grief lodge in his throat. "Yeah. Of the two of us, William was the better man. I should've been the one who died that day."

Leah placed a hand on his arm, halting their progress down the sidewalk. "You're mistaken. William wasn't the better man. Don't get me wrong; he was amazing. But so are you. You're made in God's image, and He has given you amazing gifts, Tucker. The best way to honor William's death is to seek out your purpose in this world and live it."

His breath hitched. Tucker scanned her face for any hint of deception, but there was none. Leah meant every word she was saying, and some wall surrounding his heart, built by time and sorrow, cracked. No one—not even his father—had told Tucker he was special. Pop had been a good man, but emotions were never his strong suit. Tucker hadn't realized how much impact the words would have until Leah said them out loud.

He was special. Put on earth for a purpose.

Is that true, God?

In his heart, Tucker knew it was. Memories flashed in his mind in rapid succession. All the times Pop had encouraged Tucker to attend church, William talking for hours about his faith, the guys—Nathan, Jason, and the others—gently encouraging him to seek out his purpose. And now Leah. God had been trying to reach him for years, but Tucker had been too stubborn to see it.

He'd been floating through life since returning stateside. Enrolling in college classes had been more of a band-aid than a calling. It was painful to realize he'd been wasting William's sacrifice by not seeking out his purpose. That stopped right now. "I've been a foolish man."

"God doesn't hold grudges." Leah threaded her arm through his and they continued walking. "I hope, after all this, you consider us friends because I do. How many times have you saved my life? Twice. I think once more and you get a free ice cream cone."

He laughed, pulling her closer to his side. Tucker liked having her near. Her hand was delicate and distinctly feminine against his forearm. The scent of her lavender perfume filled his senses. "We're definitely friends. And I'm pretty sure I've earned my free ice cream already. You punched me at the lake when I tried to save you."

Leah's cheeks flushed. "Whatever. I'm sure it was like being hit by a fly."

"Don't discount your punch." He rubbed his bearded jaw and grinned down at her. "You've got a mean right hook."

They laughed together.

Tucker held the door open to the police department, and they stepped inside the cool building. Chief Sam Garcia was standing at the front desk, speaking to his receptionist. His uniform was sharply pressed, black shoes shined to perfection. Mid-fifties, he took his job as police chief very seriously. He was careful, thorough, and kind. Tucker had a lot of respect for the older man.

Chief Garcia caught sight of them, murmured a few last words to his receptionist, and crossed the lobby to greet them. "Leah. Tucker. Good to see you both."

"We need to speak to you about Cory." Leah adjusted her glasses. "It's important."

The chief didn't seem surprised by her request. He escorted them to his office, and once they were seated in the visitor's chairs, he closed the door for privacy. "What's going on?"

"I know you've been investigating Cory for dealing drugs. And I know Kaylee was the person who turned him in."

The chief sighed and lowered himself into his chair. It creaked in protest. The lines bracketing his mouth deepened, making him appear older and weary. "I can't share information about an active case. What I can tell you is that Cory is a person of interest in the attacks against you." His expression turned grim. "I'd advise you to steer clear of him, Leah."

"Too late, I'm afraid. He already threatened me in the parking lot of the vet clinic this morning."

Leah ran through the incident while Chief Garcia took notes. He tossed his pen down when she was done, a frustrated expression on his face. "I'm short-staffed, but I'm going to assign a patrol officer to keep an eye on Cory. Unfortunately, it'll mean pulling the one making patrols around your neighborhood."

"That's not a problem," Tucker said. "I've made arrangements with Nathan and the others to guard Leah's property. We won't let anyone get close to her."

The chief nodded. "I was hoping that's what you'd say. Any of you boys want to join the police force, I'd be happy to have you. You've more than proven yourselves over the last few years." He scraped a hand through his gray and brown hair. "What is going on in my town? Drug dealing and disappearances. We had that incident with Cassie's stalker last year. When I was a boy, Knoxville was a quiet place. The worst thing we dealt with were speeders on Main Street."

"We're lucky to have you, Chief." Leah offered him a supportive smile. "Can you tell me anything else about the investigation into Cory?"

"No. I'm working with Detective Walsh, and he wants this to be by the book. But if Cory approaches you again, call me immediately. And you might think about taking out a restraining order against him. I'll put in a word with the judge if you choose to go that route."

"Thank you, sir. I'll consider it."

Frustration nipped at Tucker. If Cory was responsible for the attacks on Leah, he wouldn't abide by a restraining order. Worse, they could be looking in the wrong direction. He might not be involved at all. They couldn't even be certain Kaylee's disappearance was the motive for wanting Leah dead.

One thing was sure. It was only a matter of time before the assailant struck again.

ELEVEN

Leah set a basket of rolls on the table and stepped back. She eyed the men standing around the grill on her back porch. All of them former military, all of them massive eaters. She'd never hosted a dinner at her home before and nerves jittered her stomach. "I don't know. Do you think we have enough food?"

Cassie laughed. Her pretty blonde hair was pulled into a ponytail that accented her high cheekbones. "There isn't a spare inch of space on that table, and the guys are still grilling the steaks and burgers. I'd say, yes, we have enough food."

"They eat like bears coming out of hibernation."

"Worst case, we can always order extra burgers from a fast-food place." Cassie slung an arm around Leah's waist. "Don't worry. The guys eat a lot, but they're easygoing. No one is judging your dinner-party skills." Her expression grew pensive. "Have you heard from your mom?"

"No, and I've been calling her all day. I thought about going to her house, but Tucker talked me out of it. He was afraid Cory would be there. Walker did a drive-by instead." Walker Montgomery was

Tucker's friend and a former Navy SEAL. Tall and handsome, he had the muscles of a linebacker and the humor of the class clown. "He said her vehicle was in the carport, but no one was home."

It was concerning. Her mom had gone dark before, but considering Cory's behavior this morning, Leah was especially worried about her. She said a silent prayer for her mom's safety for what felt like the hundredth time.

The back door opened, bringing with it summer air, heavy with the scent of grilled meat. Tucker strolled over the threshold. He'd run home this afternoon to take a shower and grab a bag of clothes. His beard was neatly trimmed, drawing attention to the curve of his mouth and the strength of his features. A polo shirt strained to contain his muscles.

He stole her breath. For a moment, Leah was tempted to cross the room, wrap her arms around his waist, and rest her head against his chest. She envisioned his lips meeting hers. A flush crept up her neck into her cheeks as she tried to shake the images from her mind. There was nothing romantic between them. What was wrong with her?

"Burgers are done." Tucker lifted the plate in his hand. "Where should I put them?"

Their gazes met. Leah stood motionless, unable to join two thoughts together in her mind. He'd asked her a question, but she couldn't quite remember what it was. She was too busy trying to stamp down the runaway thoughts crowding her mind. Romantic dinners and quiet talks on the porch. Eating ice cream together. Heavens, she needed to date more. Something was seriously *wrong* with her.

Cassie stepped around Leah, taking the plate from Tucker. "I'll take that. Thanks. Are the steaks done?"

"Not yet. We need five minutes." Tucker frowned. Concern flickered through his eyes. "Leah, are you okay? Did something happen?"

"No." It came out on a squeak. She cleared her throat. "No, I'm good. Just tired."

"Yeah, it's been a long day." He jutted a thumb over his shoulder. "I'd better get out there before those guys burn the food. Not one of them understands how to work a grill."

Leah tilted her head to glance out the window and had to bite her lip to keep from laughing. Nathan wore an apron with the words Kiss the Chef written across the front. He was in deep conversation with his cousin Kyle, who wouldn't have looked out of place in a Western movie with his black cowboy hat and Wranglers. Both were studying the grill with concentrated effort. Logan, a former Air Force medic, had his arms crossed over his broad chest and was shouting something about fires and burns while Walker waved off his concern with a flick of the tongs. Jason, a former Marine, wisely kept out of the fray. He stood nearby, petting his dog Connor. The German shepherd panted in the heat.

They were a motley crew, obviously clueless about grilling as Tucker had said, but put any of them in a dangerous situation and it was a different story. Leah had seen the group work together when Cassie was in danger. They'd saved her best friend's life more than once. Leah was in very capable hands and grateful for every one of the men who'd volunteered to protect her.

A flame rose from the grill and Tucker bolted for the porch, the screen door slamming behind him. Cassie laughed. "Do you think we'll have to eat blackened steaks?"

Leah chuckled. "No. Tucker will save them."

Even as she spoke, Tucker grabbed the tongs out of Walker's hand and shoved the man aside. The sound of good-natured ribbing between them filtered through the closed back door. Coconut and Jax ran through the doggie door to join Connor. The three of them started running and rolling in the grass.

"So..." Cassie wriggled her eyebrows. "You and Tucker, huh? I always thought there was a spark between the two of you."

"Don't start." Leah's cheeks flushed. "Nothing is going on. We're friends."

"I don't know any friends that look at each other the way you just did a few moments ago." Cassie's brow wrinkled. "You're allowed to be happy, Leah. Tucker's a great guy."

"I know he is. It's...complicated." She busied herself with wiping crumbs off the counter. "I haven't gotten the tests results back from the doctor yet. It's not fair to pursue something with Tucker until I know for sure what's going on. He knows I've had cancer, but I didn't explain all the nitty-gritty details. And I didn't tell him that I'm waiting for my five-year checkup results."

"Leah..." Her friend's voice was sympathetic.

Cassie was aware of Leah's scars, both the visible and invisible ones. Surgery had changed her physically. Chemo had stolen Leah's ability to have children. She was grateful to be alive. She was. But the cost was high.

Leah shook her head. "Let me handle this my own way, Cass. There's a lot going on at the moment. Friendship is all I can handle right now."

Cassie was quiet for a long moment. "Okay, let me say this one thing and we won't talk about it again." She placed a hand on Leah's arm, halting her busywork. "Nathan held back his fears and worries during our first engagement under the misguided notion that he was protecting me. He was wrong. It took us far too long to realize how important being truthful with each other was. Don't make our mistake. Tell Tucker how you're feeling and about your fears."

It was good advice. But what if Tucker decided he couldn't handle all the baggage she came with? Leah didn't know if she was in the headspace to gracefully accept his rejection. "I'll think about it."

The doorbell rang and Cassie ran to answer it. She reappeared moments later with Addison, Jason's wife, and Sierra Lyons, Kyle's fiancée. Both women carried covered dishes, which they set on the table before greeting Leah with a hug.

"Where's Daniel?" Leah asked Sierra. The dark-haired beauty

was raising her nephew after her sister and brother-in-law's untimely death. Daniel was a sweet little boy with a dimpled smile who looked a lot like his aunt.

"With Kyle's mom. Gerdie offered to babysit him tonight so Kyle and I could have a kid-free dinner." Sierra winked. "And who am I to argue with my future mother-in-law?"

Leah laughed. "Knowing Gerdie, she wouldn't have taken no for an answer. She loves spending time with Daniel."

"Who could blame her? He's the cutest." Addison flashed a smile. She was dressed in a pencil skirt, silk blouse, and heels. The outfit was feminine and professional, a perfect blend for court. Addison was a family law attorney who spent her career helping women escape their abusers. Leah had spoken to her many times about her mom, and Addison had given excellent advice. Her clients were fortunate to have her.

The back door opened and the men piled inside, followed by all three dogs. Chaos reigned for the next several minutes as everyone got something to drink before choosing their seats at the table. The kitchen table wasn't designed for so many, but Nathan had brilliantly brought a board to lie across which extended the seating. Logan had brought folding chairs. It was cramped, but homey. Leah settled in her chair, her heart full. It was wonderful to have so many good friends.

Once everyone was seated, Tucker rapped on the table with his knuckles. "Okay, let's do prayer. I'll lead." He glanced at Leah. "If you don't mind. I should've asked first."

"No, please lead us." She took his hand before extending her left one to take Cassie's.

Surprise registered on several faces, but no one called attention to Tucker's unusual offer to lead prayer. In fact, there was a flicker of a smile forming on Jason's face. Leah met his gaze for half a second and the former Marine nodded before bowing his head. She had a feeling

Jason had been praying for Tucker to rediscover his faith for a long time.

"Heavenly Father, we give thanks for the food before us," Tucker said. "Please bless the hands that prepared it. We are also thankful for this wonderful group of friends. Each of us is a comfort to the other. Please watch over us all, but especially Kaylee. Lead us in the right direction and use us as Your instruments to help her. In Jesus's name, we pray. Amen."

A round of Amens followed. Leah released Cassie's hand but held onto Tucker's for a beat longer. She gently squeezed his fingers, moved beyond words that he'd included Kaylee in his prayer. It was the first moment Leah truly felt like she wasn't alone in the search for her friend. That someone else cared as much as she did.

Tucker studied their joined hands and then lifted his gaze to meet hers. A smile lifted the edges of his mouth. "Thanks for letting me lead the prayer. That felt good."

"I'm glad." She found herself smiling back.

Leah's cell phone chirped from the kitchen island. Her mom? She bolted from her chair and crossed the kitchen to grab the device. The number wasn't one she recognized. Leah swiped her phone screen to accept the call. "Hello?"

"Leah, you've made a mess of things this time." Mimi's voice was hushed and sounded loaded with tears. "Cory is furious."

Her heart rate spiked. "Mom, where are you? I've been trying to reach you all day."

Tucker rose from his chair and joined her at the island. Concern creased his brows. He placed a reassuring hand on the small of her back. His touch was comforting.

"I'm at the house," Mimi continued to whisper. "Cory took away my cell phone, but I found this extra one in his sock drawer."

Leah hurried from the kitchen toward the front door, Tucker on her heels. She grabbed her car keys from the rack. "I'm coming to get you."

"No, you can't," she hissed. "It'll just make everything worse. We need to talk. Meet me at Nelson's Diner in thirty minutes."

"Why at the diner? Why don't you come to my house?"

"It's too far. Cory's asleep now, but he'll be up soon. I want to be back home before he wakes. Thirty minutes, Leah."

Mimi hung up.

TWELVE

Nelson's Diner was on an empty stretch of country road near a gas station. The parking lot was littered with potholes and crooked blinds hung in the windows. The *e* in the neon sign flickered in distress, as if it was on the brink of going out. Leah's gaze swept across the cars scattered across the parking lot. None of them belonged to her mom. Her heart sank. "She's not here yet."

Tucker pulled into a space near the front door and killed the engine. "It hasn't been thirty minutes since she called yet. I'm sure your mom is on her way."

He was probably right. Mimi and Cory owned a house on a stretch of property on the far outskirts, near the county line, at least twenty minutes away from Nelson's. It would've taken time for her mom to slip from the house and start driving.

Tucker hopped out of the truck and circled around to open the passenger-side door. His sharp-eyed gaze swept the immediate area, his vigilance a reminder of the danger plaguing them. Leah craned her head to look out the back window. There weren't any cars coming down the country road. Where was her mom? A thousand scenarios played in her mind, each one more troubling than the last.

No. Leah wouldn't go there. It didn't help to play the what-if game. She smacked down the worry churning her stomach as Tucker opened her door and extended a hand to help her out of the vehicle. Leah slipped her fingers into his and a jolt of awareness shot through her. His hands were warm and deliciously rough with calluses. Nightfall was stealing the last of the waning sunlight. Gorgeous colors streaked across the cloudless Texas sky, providing a beautiful backdrop to the man standing in her path. His auburn beard framed a strong mouth with kissable lips. And those eyes...an emerald shade so deep Leah could become lost inside them.

Everything about Tucker made her feel safe. Which was silly. Yes, they'd known each other for months but hadn't shared more than half a dozen sentences for most of that time. It'd only been in the last two days that she and Tucker had truly gotten to know each other. It wasn't logical to have such deep feelings for someone so quickly, was it? Goodness knows, her mother fell in and out of love that fast, and those relationships had been utter disasters. Leah had prided herself on being more level-headed.

Until now.

Leah climbed out of the vehicle and quickly released Tucker's hand. If he noticed her clumsy movements, it didn't register in his expression. He hit the fob to lock the doors, and they crossed the parking lot to the diner's entrance. The scent of grilled onions and french fries made Leah's stomach rumble. She was starving. There hadn't been time to eat dinner before coming to meet Mimi.

The bells attached to the door jangled cheerily as they entered the diner. Harriet greeted them with a wide smile as she circled the front counter. She owned the diner, along with her husband, Nelson. They could've retired years ago, but cooking for weary travelers and locals gave them a reason to get up in the morning. Leah had been a frequent patron since her teenage years. She'd even waitressed for the couple while putting herself through college, and when she got cancer, Harriet and Nelson had been part of her support system. They were like surrogate grandparents.

"Leah, hon, it's so good to see you." Harriet wrapped her ample arms around Leah in a motherly embrace. "I've been so worried about you. I heard about the trouble you've been having. Did you get the pie I sent earlier today?"

"Yes, ma'am." Leah hugged the older woman back. Harriet had sent a handwritten note along with Leah's favorite dessert—a freshly baked apple pie. It'd been a kind gesture that'd brought tears to her eyes. "Thank you so much for thinking of me."

"Nonsense. It's the least I could do. If you need anything, you let me know." Harriet released her, turning to Tucker. She patted his arm in a familiar gesture. Tucker, along with the other guys in their friend group, had dinner at Nelson's every Wednesday. Harriet loved them all. "Tucker, I've got your favorite pie in the display case. Strawberry-rhubarb. Came out of the oven just a few minutes ago."

He grinned. "Give me a slice of that, please, ma'am."

Harriet chuckled. "I figured that's what you'd say. Come on, let's get you two settled at a table."

She directed them to a booth near the rear of the restaurant. Leah slid in first and Tucker took the seat next to her, so Mimi could sit across from them when she arrived. Better. Leah wanted to look her mom in the face while they talked.

Harriet took their orders, and within moments, fresh slices of pie and glasses of ice water were placed in front of them. Leah cut into the flaky crust, the scent of warm apples and cinnamon teasing her nose. She took her first bite and sighed with pleasure. "It never disappoints."

Tucker shook his head, his own fork stained red with the strawberry-rhubarb filling. "Never."

The bell over the door jangled and Mimi entered. She wore a sundress with large flowers printed across and wedge sandals. Her hair was left loose to flow over her shoulders. Dark eye-makeup was in sharp contrast to her brightly painted mouth. She spotted Leah and quickly walked to the table.

The pie turned to dust in Leah's mouth. Mimi's eyeshadow was designed to hide the purple bruise swelling along her right eye. Tucker rose to greet Mimi and Leah followed suit, intending to embrace her mom, but Mimi wasn't in the mood for her daughter's affection. She scowled and plopped down into the booth without so much as a hello. Leah retook her seat. "Would you like something to eat or drink, Mom?"

"No. My nerves are shot, but this stupid diner doesn't serve alcohol." Her hand trembled as she pushed a lock of dyed hair behind her ear. "You need to clear up this mess, Leah. I want you to tell Chief Garcia that Cory didn't have anything to do with Kaylee's disappearance."

Leah pressed her lips together to keep from blurting out the first words that came to her mind. She sent up a silent prayer to God for patience and understanding. "Mom, did you know Cory was dealing drugs?"

Mimi blinked her mascara-coated lashes, her gaze skittering away. "That's a vicious rumor. Where did you hear such gossip?"

She knew. Leah's heart tumbled to her feet. "When Kaylee was struggling with addiction, Cory was the one who sold her the drugs. She turned him in to the police."

Mimi's complexion paled. "And so what? You think he hurt her because of it?"

"I think it's possible. He hurts you regularly, and Cory threatened me this morning. He's got a temper."

"Having a temper is a far cry from what you're accusing him of." Mimi grabbed an abandoned straw wrapper from the table and twisted it in between her fingers. "You believe the person who kidnapped Kaylee is the same one who attacked you? Well, it can't be

Cory. The night that guy tried to break into your house, my husband was with me." She jutted up her chin. "Hear that, Leah. Cory was with me the entire night."

Her voice rang with sincerity, but that didn't mean much. Mimi had been drinking heavily that night. She could've fallen asleep, and Cory slipped out of the house. Leah couldn't think of a nice way to say that, so she stayed quiet. Tucker, to his credit, also didn't say anything.

"Cory is furious with you." Mimi twisted the straw wrapper around one finger and it snapped. "He doesn't like Chief Garcia accusing him of stuff. It's not true, for starters, and it isn't good for business. The junkyard pays our bills."

Leah doubted the junkyard was bringing in any significant amount of money. Mimi's inheritance check every month was likely paying the light bill. Cory didn't care one whit for Mimi, and Leah couldn't understand why her mother didn't see it.

"Like I said," Mimi continued. "You need to tell Chief Garcia that Cory didn't have anything to do with Kaylee's disappearance. If you don't do that, then we can't be a part of each other's lives anymore."

Her heart twisted hard. "Mom, please. You don't mean that."

"Yes, I do." Her painted mouth hardened. "You've gone too far this time. Cory is innocent of the accusations you've leveled against him. I won't have you smearing his good name."

His good name? Even if he didn't have anything to do with Kaylee's disappearance, Mimi was sitting across from her with a black eye. How could she continue to defend and stay with him? While Leah mentally understood the complexities of an abusive relationship, it was incredibly painful to have her own mother choose a man over her.

This wasn't like Mimi. She'd kissed Leah's skinned knees, worked two jobs to pay for math tutoring, and cheered into a blow horn when

Leah graduated high school. She'd dated losers in the past, some of whom were verbally abusive, but Mimi hit a breaking point early on with all of them. And she'd never allowed any of those boyfriends to say one bad thing about Leah, let alone lay a hand on her. Mimi's defense of Cory was like entering the twilight zone or some alternate reality.

Under the table, Tucker placed a hand on Leah's knee. His touch was gentle and grounding. A reminder that she wasn't in this alone. It gave her the strength to push aside the anger and confusion. Leah drew in a steadying breath. "Mom, I love you. I don't want you to be hurt."

"Then put this right." Mimi slid from the booth. "I've got to go before Cory realizes I'm missing."

She left in a flurry of clopping wedges. Leah watched, heart in her throat, as her mom got into a beat-up sedan and sped out of the parking lot. Their conversation played out again in her mind, as it would over the next several hours. "I didn't handle that well."

"On the contrary, I think you handled it exceptionally well." Tucker squeezed her knee. "You were compassionate and loving. That couldn't have been easy."

Leah leaned on his shoulder, tears pricking her eyes. His kindness was a balm she needed. "She knows he's selling drugs. That's scary. My mom has made bad choices before, but it's never been this awful. I don't know how to reach her."

"I don't think it's up to you. Remember what we talked about earlier today? You're a fixer, but there are some things that you have to hand over to God." His lips brushed against the top of her head. "This is one of those, Leah."

She sighed. "Was it just this morning we had that conversation? It feels like a lifetime ago."

"I know."

He wrapped his arms around her, and they sat quietly for several minutes. Leah listened to the steady beat of Tucker's heart and let it soothe her raw emotions. He was an anchor in the storm. Part of her was concerned about relying too much on him, but the other part couldn't resist. Something was happening between them. There was no denying it any longer. But was it the kind of relationship that could survive the test of time? She wasn't sure.

"We should go." Leah pulled away from Tucker, trying to put some physical and mental space between them. "Harriet's pie is wonderful, but it's not dinner. If we don't get home soon, there may not be anything left for us to eat."

"Don't worry. Cassie said she'd fix us each a plate and set them aside." He winked. "I didn't want to chance it."

"Wise man."

They slid out of the booth and paid the bill. Darkness had fallen and the parking lot was pitch-black save for a few scattered overhead lights with weak bulbs. Leah used her hand to lift the curls off the back of her neck. The air was humid, thick enough to feel like a damp curtain. "I wish this heat wave would pass. Nighttime is usually pleasant, even in the summer, but these temperatures are almost unbearable."

"Makes me grateful for air-conditioning." Tucker reached for the truck's passenger-side door, but stopped halfway. His body jolted and then dropped to the asphalt like a rag doll, his head smashing against the side of the truck on the way down. His entire body shook as if he was having a seizure.

"Tucker!" Leah dropped to her knees beside him. She was just about to turn Tucker on his side when the violent shaking stopped. His eyes were wide, and a sound came from his throat. "Help!" Leah screamed, unable to tear her gaze away from Tucker.

He made another sound through gritted teeth. Leah blinked. Run? Did he say run?

A looming figure came out of the shadows. Tucker jolted again, his body shaking violently. With horror, Leah realized they were under attack. Faint wires drifted from his hip, disappearing into the darkness. A Taser?

Tucker stopped moving and Leah ripped the prongs out of his skin. "Help! Help us!"

The looming shadow rushed her.

THIRTEEN

Move.

The command reverberated in Tucker's skull, cutting through the pain from being tased twice. He gritted his teeth. Leah's screams carried across the parking lot, spurring his movement. Blood speckled the asphalt. She'd fought with the attacker and, from the sounds of it, still was. Tucker's heart rate spiked as he gripped the side of his vehicle and struggled to a standing position. His knees wobbled as if he was a newborn calf.

A short distance away, Leah struggled with a man dressed in all black. She kicked her attacker in the knee, and he smacked her across the face in response before grabbing her by the hair. He dragged her toward a beat-up sedan. Tucker's blood boiled. He took a shaky step forward and then another. Pulling his weapon would be useless. He couldn't hit the broad side of a barn, but that wouldn't stop him from saving Leah.

She screamed, her voice carrying across the distance between them. Was it loud enough to be heard inside the diner? Tucker prayed it was the case. He would need backup. Each movement was torture, white-hot pain shooting across his head. Something dripped down his chin. Blood? Maybe. It felt like his brain was about to explode. He ground his teeth together and kept moving.

He'd failed before. He refused to fail again.

Tucker increased his speed, lowered his head, and barreled straight into the attacker. They flew a short distance before crashing to the ground in a tangle of limbs. A fist slammed into Tucker's face. He responded with a punch of his own, but the hit landed somewhere on the man's shoulder. He didn't let that stop him. Tucker kept fighting, moving, trying to get the upper hand. But his body wouldn't respond quick enough.

Had Leah run? He didn't know where she was nor could he spare a second to check.

A shout carried across the parking lot, followed by the pump of a shotgun. The attacker sprang to his feet and bolted. Tucker struggled to a sitting position as Nelson stepped into a circle of light. His apron was stained with remnants of food and he carried a shotgun. He took aim and fired at the attacker's vehicle as it raced out of the lot. Taillights faded into the night.

"Tucker!" Leah appeared at his side. Her hair flowed like a river of curls. The curves of her face were cast in light and shadow, the angles delicate and feminine. Her cheek was red from being struck, but she otherwise appeared unharmed.

Thank you, God.

She reached under his arms, as if to help him up. Tucker waved off her assistance. "I'm okay. Just wobbly from being tased."

"You've got a lump the size of a cantaloupe forming on the side of your head, son." Nelson joined them, his gaze sweeping over their forms. "And you're getting quite the bruise on your cheek, Leah. You both need some ice for those wounds. Let's get y'all inside. Harriet's already called the police. They're on the way."

Ten minutes later, they were inside the diner's rear office with a first aid kit. Tucker made sure Leah was taken care of first before wrapping his own ice pack in paper towels and pressing it to his head wound. He winced at the sharp pain. A headache was already pounding along his temple, but the pain was nothing compared to the guilt pressing down on his shoulders. He'd screwed up, and it'd nearly cost Leah her life.

"What are you thinking about so hard over there?" Leah lowered the ice pack from her cheek. "I can practically hear the wheels in your head turning."

"I was considering asking Nathan or Logan to step in as your bodyguard. What happened tonight is inexcusable. I should've been paying more attention to our surroundings."

Her eyes flashed. "Baloney. The lights in the parking lot are abysmal, and the attacker used a stun gun with some kind of long distance prongs. There's no way you could've predicted what he'd do, and you were nearly killed trying to save me."

His jaw tightened. Her words were kind, but that didn't change the facts. The red mark on her face was proof of his mistakes. "You were hurt."

"So were you." She rose from her chair and reached for the first aid kit. "In fact, you're still bleeding."

Leah ripped open a package of gauze and gestured for him to lower the ice pack. Her gaze on his wound was almost physical in its intensity as she stepped closer. The scent of her lavender bodywash enveloped him. His head swam. Not from the headache, but from her nearness. It took everything inside Tucker to keep his hands at his side instead of reaching for her waist.

She gently dabbed at his wound. Her movements were efficient, the touch of a woman practiced in caring for the injured, such as her animals. Leah cupped his chin in her hand and tilted his head to gain better access. Her touch sent a wave of molten heat through him.

"This is going to hurt tomorrow, but thankfully, it doesn't need stitches." Leah bit her lip. "I don't want Nathan or Logan to be my bodyguard. I want you, Tucker. That is...if you still want to. I wouldn't blame you for bowing out considering what happened tonight."

He took hold of her wrist and gently tugged her hand away from his chin. It was difficult to think when she was touching him. "Listen to me carefully. I've stared death in the face before and didn't blink. The danger isn't the problem. I don't want to fail you."

"You could never fail me."

His breath hitched as the impact of her words slammed into him with the force of a bullet. Their gazes met. Something earth-shattering was buried in the depths of her dark eyes. Something that Tucker knew deep down would change his life forever. It was terrifying and exhilarating. And absolutely illogical given the time they'd spent together.

Or maybe it wasn't. He'd been more vulnerable—more real—with Leah than he'd ever been with anyone. With her, he could just...be. It was profound, and if he was being honest, Tucker had sensed this brewing connection from the first moment he'd met her. He'd fought against it, but there was no escaping the truth.

Her gaze dropped to his mouth. The air surrounding them electrified.

"Leah..." He whispered her name, in warning or invitation Tucker couldn't say. But if she kept looking at him like that, he wasn't going to be able to resist kissing her.

He didn't have a chance to decide. She leaned down and pressed her lips gently to his. The world tilted on its axis and all sense of reason fled as Tucker rose from the chair to take her into his arms. He buried his hands in those gorgeous locks and tilted her head to deepen the kiss. She tasted like apple pie and sweetness and everything good in the world. He wanted to drown in her touch.

It was physically painful to end the kiss. Tucker brushed his lips against hers once more before pulling back to regain his breath. Leah appeared stunned. It was a sentiment he shared.

Before he could find his voice, a sharp knock came on the door. It had the effect of being doused with cold water. Leah backed out of his embrace, putting an appropriate distance between them seconds before the door swung open.

Detective Walsh strolled in. His expression was grim, his hair mussed as if he'd been running his hands through it. Sweat beaded on his forehead. "Either of you need an ambulance?"

"No, sir." Tucker ran through what happened while the detective took notes on a small pad. "I didn't get a solid look at the attacker. He was wearing all black and a ski mask, but his height and weight were approximately the same as the man I chased away from Leah's house the other night."

Detective Walsh mopped his brow with a handkerchief. "What about the vehicle? Did you see a license plate?"

He shook his head. "It was too dark."

"That's what Nelson said." He turned his attention to Leah. "Anything to add?"

She gingerly touched her face. "He didn't kill me. There was time after..." Her gaze darted toward Tucker before landing back on the detective. "The attacker could've shot me, but he didn't. Instead, he tried to kidnap me and I don't understand why."

The same question had been rolling through Tucker's mind repeatedly in a loop. It didn't make sense. The attacker at the lake had nearly drowned Leah. The point was to kill her. Were they dealing with two different individuals? If so, what did that mean for their investigation into Kaylee's disappearance?

Detective Walsh frowned. "What's your relationship like with Cory?"

"Difficult. We don't like each other much." Her eyes widened. "You don't think he could've..."

Detective Walsh was silent, but Tucker didn't need him to explain. He hated the idea of Mimi's involvement—for Leah's sake—but he couldn't ignore the potential. Tucker took Leah's hand, knowing this would be hard for her to hear. "Your house is protected by a group of trained ex-military members. Your mom's phone call might've been designed to lure you to the diner."

Pain rippled across her pretty features. She ripped her hand from his and took a step backward. "My mom has her faults—I won't deny it—but she'd never agree to something like that."

Her response was immediate, and the strength of her conviction rang clear. Tucker didn't know Mimi well, and family members rarely believed a relative would cause them harm, but Leah had been forthright about her mother's shortcomings. He reconsidered. "What if she didn't know? Cory could've *fallen asleep*," Tucker used air quotes around fallen asleep, "and waited to see what Mimi would do. He might've been listening in on the phone conversation and followed her here."

Her spine softened. "That's true."

Detective Walsh clicked his pen closed. "Either way, I'll question Cory tonight. I suggest the two of you head home and sit tight for the time being. I'll call you if there are any updates."

Leah put out a hand to stop him. "And Kaylee's case? Are you reopening it? Cory had a reason to hurt her. She'd turned him into the police for dealing drugs."

"Cory has been questioned and his place searched regarding the drug accusation. Nothing was found. Either Kaylee was lying about who her dealer was or Cory got out of the business before she turned him in." Detective Walsh tucked his pad into the top pocket of his suit jacket. "Cory had no reason to hurt or kidnap Kaylee. As for her case, it's still an active investigation. If new information comes up, it'll be pursued."

Heat washed through Tucker's veins as his temper rose. "So you still don't believe these attacks could be linked to Kaylee's disappearance? I can understand keeping an open mind, but you're outright rejecting a possible motive."

"I don't work on supposition. I work on facts." He pinned them with a glare. "Let me give you some free advice. It's not wise to go around town asking questions. Folks get real nervous that you're gonna start accusing them of things they didn't do. Leave the investigating to the professionals."

Tucker crossed his arms over his chest. He didn't take kindly to Detective Walsh making declarations. The man had dismissed Kaylee's case from the start. It was frustrating and more than a bit confounding. Unless...was it possible the detective was covering for someone? Or knew more about the case than he was saying?

A chill crept across Tucker's skin. He didn't like the turns his thoughts were taking. "We want answers about what happened to Kaylee, Detective Walsh."

"Sometimes there aren't any." His tone was cold and his gaze hard. "I'm telling you to let it go before y'all end up in a grave."

FOURTEEN

Leah cuddled Coconut on her lap with one hand while she stroked Jax's head with the other. The Lab-mix had nestled up next to her on the couch, his weighty head resting on her leg, his dark eyes pools of sympathy and understanding. The dogs didn't know why she was stressed, but they could sense her unease and wanted to comfort her. It was pure love. Exactly the medicine she needed.

Was Cory trying to kill her? Did he kidnap and potentially harm Kaylee? Did her mother know? Leah had defended Mimi confidently at the diner, but in the hours since then, doubt had niggled its way past her convictions. After all, her mom knew about the drugs. What else had she been keeping from her daughter? It was too horrifying to contemplate.

God, I don't know where this is going, but I need you now more than ever. My heart feels like it's on the verge of breaking. I've been so strong, held it together through the cancer and Kaylee's disappearance, but this...this feels bigger than I can handle.

The back door opened and Tucker strolled inside. The fluorescent lights in the kitchen played off the strong angles of his face and the brighter red highlights in his beard. Leah's pulse pounded as the memory of the kiss they'd shared flooded over her. It'd been a reckless move on her part. With so much going on—the investigation into Kaylee's disappearance, the attacks, her upcoming oncology visit—it was a terrible time to begin a romantic relationship. But logic didn't always play a part when emotions were involved. Something had been brewing between them for a while and fighting it wasn't working. In fact, it was exhausting.

It also went against everything Leah promised herself when her cancer went into remission. Each day was a gift. She'd sworn to make her slice of the world better and to live fearlessly. Rescuing animals, her volunteer work with the church, and finding Kaylee were part of that. But Leah had held back when it came to her feelings for Tucker. It was wrong, and it'd taken him nearly dying for her to realize it.

But now...now she needed to have a hard conversation with him.

Tucker came into the living room on silent feet, spotted her on the couch with the dogs, and smiled softly. "I wondered why Jax didn't greet me at the door. He's getting loved on."

At the sound of his name, Jax raised his head slightly and thumped his tail in greeting but didn't budge from Leah's side. Coconut cracked one eye to assess the situation and then settled back on her pillow with a sigh of contentment. Leah grinned. "Some guard dogs, huh?"

"That's okay. We've got things covered. Logan and Walker are taking the first shift tonight."

Leah's gaze drifted to the window near the couch. It was pitch-black outside, the moon hidden behind a wall of clouds. Thunderstorms were predicted for tomorrow. "Did you mention they're welcome to come inside at any time? For coffee or snacks, or even to use the bathroom?"

"I did." Tucker folded his tall form into an armchair and stretched his legs out in front of him. His feet were clad in socks. The intimacy of having him in her home late at night wasn't lost on Leah. Nor was the feeling of security he gave her. "Don't worry, Leah. The guys are used to roughing it." He waved a hand around the room. "This is a palace compared to some of the places we've been."

"These last few days have been nerve-racking. I can't imagine being in a war zone, constantly facing danger all the time."

"You get used to it, in a way. You have to in order to get your job done. It's coming home that can really mess with your mind." He was quiet for a long moment. "I changed overseas and nothing felt the same anymore."

She could relate to that. Stepping out of the hospital after receiving the news she was officially in remission had been strangely bizarre. Leah had fought for so long to get healthy that once she was, she'd forgotten what it was like to be normal. Cassie had been the one to support her through it. "It helps to have good friends, doesn't it?"

"Absolutely. I give thanks every day for these guys."

Silence settled between them. The fridge kicked on, mixing with the hum of the air conditioner. Nerves jittered her stomach. She needed to address the elephant in the room. Waiting would only make things harder. "We should talk about what happened tonight. About the kiss."

Something in her voice must've betrayed her uncertainty, because Tucker sat up straighter in his chair. He lifted a hand to stop her. "There's one thing I have to say before we start. I understand things are complicated right now, but I don't regret what happened between us." His lips curved into a heartbreaking smile. "Not even for a minute. I hope you don't either."

She licked her lips and stroked Jax's head. "It's complicated. I have feelings for you, Tucker, but..."

Gosh, this was so much harder than she'd thought it would be to say out loud. Did she really have to tell him? After all, it was just one kiss. She wouldn't explain these things on a first date.

No. That wasn't a fair comparison. What was happening between her and Tucker ran deep. The intensity of their kiss was proof of that. He'd already suffered so much with the death of

William and his father. It wasn't right to continue without being honest. She owed it to him and to herself.

Leah sucked in a deep breath. "There's a lot of baggage the cancer left me with. For starters, there are scars. And I can't have kids." She blinked back tears. "My cancer is in remission, but I need checkups every year. This is my fifth one, and it's critical. If the cancer stays away, then my chances of living a long, healthy life improve dramatically. But if it's come back..."

She didn't want to voice what would happen next. "I haven't spoken to my doctor about the results yet. She's supposed to call me in a few days. Normally, I wouldn't say anything, but then I went and kissed you." Leah smiled weakly but couldn't quite bring herself to meet his eyes. "I probably shouldn't have done that, and I understand completely if you want to put whatever is happening on ice."

Tucker rose from the chair and gently pushed Jax aside so he could sit on the couch. He took hold of her chin and turned her head until she was forced to look into his face. Leah's breath stalled at the depth of emotion in his gaze. There wasn't pity or fear. There was only warmth and affection and a hint of something far greater...not love, but something close to it.

"I don't want to stop what's happening between us. Not for a second. Thank you for telling me about your worries, but you aren't the only one who comes with baggage. I can be quiet and broody." He took her hand and placed it on his chest. The thump of his heart beat against her palm. "I have scars of my own. My renewed relationship with God is rocky. I don't have a permanent home and have no idea what my career is going to be after I'm done with college." He cocked a smile. "Personally, I think you should be the one away from me."

"So where does that leave us?"

"How about taking things one day at a time?" Tucker leaned forward and brushed his lips against hers. "This thing between us feels right. I want to see where it takes us." He pulled back to look her in the eyes. "What do you want?"

She wanted to take a flying leap into his arms, but while Leah was fearless, she wasn't completely reckless. Her mother's pattern of relationships had taught her the prudence of being cautious with her heart. Things were heightened right now. For both of them. Making promises or declarations wasn't a good idea. She'd said her piece and it was enough for the moment. "One day at a time sounds perfect to me."

He gave her a heart-stopping smile. Leah found herself grinning back. Cleaning the air between them had lifted an immense weight from her shoulders. She leaned into his embrace until her cheek was resting against his chest. Jax joined them, putting his head on Tucker's leg this time. It was cozy and sweet and the perfect antidote to the worries plaguing her mind. "I haven't heard from Detective Walsh yet. And my mom isn't answering her phone again."

Tucker trailed his fingers across the bruise on her cheek. His touch was butterfly soft. "Nathan's on his way to their house to check things out. He left about twenty minutes ago. I'll let you know the moment he reports in."

Leah breathed out a sigh of relief. "Was that your idea?" She didn't need him to answer. It was obvious. "Thank you, Tucker."

"No need to thank me, sweetheart. She's your mom. You love her and that makes protecting her as much as we can a priority for me."

This man. There was no defense strong enough to keep Tucker from stealing her heart if he kept this up. No one—not even her mother—had ever made her feel safe and cherished. Until now. It was heady and intoxicating, and Leah never wanted it to end.

She lifted her head and was about to press a kiss to Tucker's lips when his cell phone beeped. He held up a finger. "Hold that thought." Then he unhooked the device from his belt and checked the message. Tucker frowned. "Holt Alder is heading up your walkway to the front porch. Were you expecting him?"

Leah straightened. "No."

The doorbell rang. Jax and Coconut sprang into action, bounding from the couch and racing for the entryway, fierce barks alerting the visitor of their presence. Tucker followed, his long strides eating up the distance with ease.

Leah commanded the dogs to sit, and they complied. Then she opened the door. "Holt, hi."

The veterinarian shifted in his tennis shoes. He wore surgical scrubs, as if he was heading home from work, and the dark circles under his eyes were a testament to the long hours he put in. As the only vet in the county, Holt often worked late or early in the morning. Leah always called his office ahead of time to schedule an appointment and she'd had several canceled at the last minute because of a calving emergency or a sick horse.

Holt offered her a weak smile. "Hey, Leah. Sorry to drop by unexpectedly, but I need to talk to you. Mind if I come in?"

"Not at all." Leah stepped back so he could cross the threshold. She escorted him to the living room, shushing Jax along the way. The dog really didn't like the vet much. Curiosity was nagging Leah about his impromptu visit, but she kept it at bay. Manners first. "Can I get you some coffee? Or iced tea? You look like you need either a dose of caffeine or a day's worth of sleep."

"Iced tea would be great."

She rounded up his drink while Holt greeted Tucker and attempted to make nice with the dogs. Coconut happily accepted his ministrations, but Jax kept a wary distance. Leah smiled at the way her lab sidled up to Tucker for comfort. The tough Army Ranger didn't disappoint. He gently stroked Jax's head to reassure him.

Leah handed Holt his drink before sitting across from him on the couch. "Everything okay?"

Holt twisted the ice tea in his hands. His posture was rigid, his shoulders tight. Tucker remained standing but out of Holt's direct eyesight. Was that on purpose? Leah was inclined to believe so. She met Tucker's gaze briefly, and he nodded as if to encourage her to focus on Holt.

The vet took a drink. "I've been thinking a lot about what we discussed in my office yesterday. About Kaylee's disappearance."

Leah held her breath and stayed quiet, sensing this would be easier if Holt guided the conversation. Coconut tugged at her pant leg and she lifted the pup into her lap. The act was rewarded with a kiss on the wrist.

Holt shifted uncomfortably in the chair and then raked a hand through his blond locks. "I debated saying something for a long time. Even thought about telling Chief Garcia, but..." He licked his lips and raised his gaze to Leah's. "You need to understand. When Cassie had trouble with that stalker, I was a suspect. Can you imagine how awful that felt? I don't want to accuse someone without cause."

Sympathy tugged at Leah. Knoxville was a small town, with all the joys and trials that went with it. "I do understand, Holt. All I want is the truth. I'm not interested in tarnishing anyone's reputation."

Her words seemed to reassure him. Holt set his glass on the coffee table. "A few days before Kaylee disappeared, she had a run-in with a new customer. Enzo Murray. He'd brought his pit bull into the office, claiming the dog had hurt himself on a chain-link fence. The dog's face and ear were sliced. There were old scars on him as well. Kaylee suspected the animal was being used for dog fighting and said so."

That was just like Kaylee. She loved animals and wouldn't mince words if she suspected one was being injured by the owner.

Enzo Murray wasn't a name Leah recognized, but the town had been growing rapidly in recent years. She didn't know every resident anymore. "Dog fighting is illegal in Texas. Depending on the offense, it can carry up to twenty years in jail."

"Yep, and Enzo knew it. He became enraged and stormed out of our office." Holt winced. "He threatened Kaylee. At the time, I considered it a passing comment from an angry man, but then..."

"Then she disappeared." Leah finished for him. She lifted her gaze to Tucker. "There have been rumors of dog fighting recently. Several pit bulls have ended up at the shelter after being dumped, their injuries consistent with a bad tussle. Kaylee wasn't the kind to stay quiet about animal abuse. If Enzo suspected she was planning on turning him into the police—"

"He could've made a plan to silence her." He grimaced. "For good."

FIFTEEN

The next morning, the sky was thick with thunderclouds. Rain battered the kitchen windowpane. Tucker poured himself a cup of coffee—his third for the day—and grabbed a slice of bacon from a plate in the center of the table. He didn't feel like eating but knew from his time in the military that food was fuel. He couldn't operate at his best without it.

He selected a chair next to Leah. Shadows marred the delicate skin under her eyes. She hadn't slept well. Neither had Tucker. The attack yesterday—along with her mother's potential involvement—had left a sour taste in his mouth. He'd considered getting an update from the guys without her but, ultimately, decided that wasn't fair. This was her life. She deserved to know what was going on.

Tucker bit into the bacon with more force than was necessary. "What's the update, Nathan?"

"Cops were crawling all over the Olsens' place last night." His gaze darted to Leah, concern flickering in the depths of his eyes. "I asked Chief Garcia this morning about it. Cory and Mimi were both questioned, but nothing came of it."

Leah's fingers shook as she reached for her mug. "I don't know if that's good news or bad. Of course, I don't want my mom in trouble. But Cory is a different matter. I'm sure he's beating her and I find it hard to believe Kaylee was lying about who her drug dealer was. There's no reason for her to."

Tucker agreed with her assessment. He wasn't taking Cory off the suspect list. Not by a long shot. "Jason, what have you uncovered about Cory?"

"Not much. Most people weren't willing to talk to me about him." Jason rubbed the scar streaking across his face. The injury had come from an IUD blast. Connor, his German shepard, also had a scar cutting through his fur. The dog was resting under the table with Jax and Coconut. All three appeared to be waiting for someone to drop a morsel or two. "Cory has been arrested for a few minor infractions, but nothing stuck. Depending on who you talk to, he's either a good old country boy or a rebel without a cause. His junkyard isn't making much money. The property he and Mimi live in was inherited from his grandpa. Before marrying Mimi, Cory dated a string of women. Most of them didn't have nice things to say about him. He drinks too much, is jealous, and has a tendency to talk with his fists when mad."

Leah paled, but her voice was composed when she asked, "What about dealing drugs?"

"I need to ask around more. People can be slow to admit when they're doing something illegal, even to another civilian."

Tucker mulled that over. "Detective Walsh believes Cory might've gotten out of the business before Kaylee turned him in. I wonder if he caught wind of her intentions before she could turn him into the police."

"It would give Cory a motive to silence her," Jason pointed out. "If his main source of income is drugs, then he could've taken a hiatus until the heat wore off. He gets rid of Kaylee and starts again."

"Good point. I definitely don't want to take him off the suspect list, but he isn't the only one with motive to get rid of Kaylee."

"Agreed. Enzo Murray is bad news." Kyle slid a folder across the table. The former Army security specialist was a trained hacker with a knack for background checks. "He's got a rap sheet longer than my arm for assault, robbery, and animal abuse."

Tucker set aside his coffee and opened the folder to review the documents. He whistled. "Enzo is twenty-seven years old, and he's been arrested numerous times since his eighteenth birthday."

"Yep. Did a stint in jail for assaulting a guy in a bar with a knife, but got out early for good behavior. He's also spent some time in county lockup here and there, but most of those charges were pled out." Kyle shoveled scrambled eggs onto his fork. "For all the trouble Enzo's been in, he hasn't done much time in lockup."

Nathan crossed his arms over his chest. "Forgive me for being the naysayer here, but I don't trust Holt Adler as far as I can throw him. That man threatened Cassie not too long ago. He wasn't her stalker, but that doesn't mean he's a good guy. How can we be sure he isn't sending us on a wild goose chase?"

Tucker reared back. "You think Holt had something to do with Kaylee's disappearance?"

"I spoke to the Grangers. They confirmed Holt was on their property the night Kaylee disappeared, but can't confirm the time he left. I wouldn't strike him from the suspect list so quickly or trust the information he provides."

"Hold on," Walker held up his hand, his Southern drawl thick with fatigue. He'd been up all night, keeping guard over Leah's house with Logan. After breakfast, he'd be heading to bed for some shut-eye. "We thoroughly investigated Holt when Cassie was threatened. The women he'd dated mentioned he was intense, but none of them felt threatened by him. He's never been arrested. No one has a bad thing to say about him."

Nathan raised a brow. "No one had a bad thing to say about Ted Bundy either, and he was a serial killer."

"Point taken."

"He asked Kaylee out a few times." Leah's voice was soft, a frown pulling down the corners of her mouth. "She refused, and then Holt stopped. But there was an energy about him whenever she was in the room. It always bothered me."

Instinct. It wasn't something to be dismissed, in Tucker's opinion. Leah had initially suspected Holt, and while Nathan had a good reason to dislike the vet, it didn't make his point invalid. Was Holt hiding a dark side? It was worth considering.

Tucker turned to Kyle. "Can you do a deeper dive into Holt? Maybe talk to some people he knew in vet school or even college?"

"Absolutely."

"In the meantime, Enzo is someone we should follow up with. If he had an altercation with Kaylee at the vet's office, that should be easy to confirm."

"I'll go with you to speak to him," Nathan said.

Leah pushed aside her plate. "I'd like to go too."

Tucker frowned. "That's not a good idea. If Enzo sees us with you, he's likely to refuse to talk. Guys like him do better when it's man to man. Besides, it's safer for you at the house. Jason and Connor are going to take the morning shift. You won't be alone for a minute."

Leah opened her mouth as if to argue but seemed to think better of it. "Okay. I'll stay back. There's a pile of paperwork from the shelter to take care of anyway." She rose from her chair and glanced around the table. "In case I haven't said it before, thanks, guys. What you're doing to help me, to help Kaylee, means the world to me."

"Don't give it a minute's thought." Nathan scooped her up into a brotherly hug. "This group sticks together through thick and thin." He set her back down on her feet. "Besides, if I let anything happen to you, my wife would hurt me."

Leah laughed. It was warm and sweet. There was no romantic connection between her and Nathan, yet Tucker felt an unusual spark of jealousy when the other guys also hugged her and offered reassurance. It was distinctly uncomfortable. He'd had relationships before but avoided diving into anything serious. His job as an Army Ranger, and all the deployments that came with it, had provided an easy out. Tucker also hadn't considered himself marriage material.

Now, things were different. Leah was different.

Their conversation last night replayed in his mind repeatedly. It haunted him. She'd mentioned her cancer struggle before, but Tucker hadn't realized the extent of her battle. The scars didn't bother him. Nor did the infertility. His father had been adopted and always spoke so lovingly of his parents. No, it was the upcoming test results that terrified him the most.

Would he save Leah from a killer only to lose her to cancer?

And was he strong enough to hold her hand through it, if that was the case?

He hadn't been there for his dad. It was a source of hurt and deep regret. His aunt swore Pops kept his cancer a secret so Tucker wouldn't derail his career. But secretly, he'd always wondered if his father believed Tucker wasn't capable of handling his diagnosis.

After breakfast cleanup, Leah joined him on the porch to say goodbye. He brushed a kiss across her cheek, breathing in the scent of her lavender shampoo. It was torture to leave her, but Jason would protect her with his life. Tucker had no doubt about it.

Nathan fired up his truck and pulled out of the driveway. He shot a quick glance toward Tucker. "What's going on with you and Leah?"

The question was heavy with accusation, but Tucker didn't take it personally. He'd known this conversation was coming from the moment Nathan mentioned interviewing Enzo together. It was an opportunity to speak alone. Nathan was protective of Leah and acted as her surrogate older brother. He wouldn't tolerate her being played with.

"I care about her." Tucker adjusted the air-conditioning vent. "We care about each other. Where it's going. I'm not sure, but I can promise that I have no intention of hurting her."

Nathan's hand tightened on the steering wheel. "She's been

through a lot, man. Matters of the heart can get messy." He shot him another dark glance. "And you've never showed interest in marriage. I understand how feelings can develop during dangerous times, but Leah will need someone long after this threat is over. She deserves the best."

His words poked at a hidden sore spot. Tucker had failed his father by staying in the military after Pop got cancer. He failed to protect William from a bullet. He'd failed to keep Cassie's surrogate brother from being kidnapped by her stalker last year. And yesterday he'd screwed up and it'd nearly cost Leah her life. "Anyone but me, huh?"

The words came out harsh and filled with anger. Tucker tightened his hold on the roll bar and diverted his gaze out the window. Pine trees whipped by in a blur. He'd known Nathan would have reservations, but it stung to hear them said out loud.

"Tucker...man. This isn't easy for me to say. I'd trust you with my life—"

"Just not with Leah's heart."

"Don't make this harder than it has to be. I'm watching out for her." Nathan's jaw tightened. "This isn't meant to be insulting."

"Well, it is." Tucker spun in his seat. "You literally broke up with Cassie on your wedding day, and yet when things started developing between the two of you again, I didn't say one word against it. I trusted you to know your own feelings and to treat her with respect."

"That's not the same. You didn't know Cassie well. Leah's like my little sister." He exited the freeway and pulled into a rest stop before shoving the vehicle into Park and facing Tucker. "I see the way she looks at you. It's not an infatuation on her part. Her heart is getting involved, and that's something you have to take seriously."

"I am," he roared. The depth of his anger shocked him and Tucker fumbled with the door handle before exiting the truck. He wanted to simultaneously punch something and run a thousand miles until his emotions were under control.

He felt, rather than heard, Nathan get out of the vehicle. Tucker sucked in a deep breath, drawing on his training to temper his voice and cool his emotions. "She has a doctor's appointment coming up. Five-year cancer check. She's terrified." His chest constricted as his voice broke. "Leah would never say so, but I can tell she's scared. I don't know how to help her. All I can do is protect her from this lunatic trying to kill her."

"You're falling in love with her."

"Is that what this is? This sick, panicked feeling that won't let up." Tucker snorted. "It's not how they portray it in the movies. Why would anyone sign up for this?"

Nathan chuckled. "We don't. It just...happens. And nothing in this world is better than having the woman you love return the feeling." He grew quiet for a long moment. "It's also terrifying to put your heart in someone else's hands. Especially if you've never done it before. I'm sorry, Tucker. I didn't realize the depth of your feelings for Leah."

Tucker shook his head. "No, you're right to question me. I got mad because you have a point. I'm a screw-up, Nathan. What if I can't be the man she deserves?"

"We're all screw-ups." Nathan's mouth tilted up. "As you aptly pointed out, I literally left Cassie at the altar." He clapped a hand on Tucker's shoulder. "Yes, Leah is scared about the upcoming doctor's visit and these threats against her don't help, but being by her side means more than you know. So does prayer. Whatever concerns and worries you're having, give them to God."

"I haven't been very good about that lately. I've been pretty angry with Him."

"That's okay. He doesn't hold grudges."

Tucker chuckled. "Leah told me exactly the same thing."

"She's smart." Nathan dropped his hand. "Now that we aren't going to punch each other out, ready to talk to Enzo?"

"Yep. Let's go."

SIXTEEN

Enzo worked at a car mechanic shop just off the freeway. He was outside taking a smoke break when Nathan pulled into the parking lot. The man looked exactly like his most recent booking photo. Long unkempt black hair swept his shoulders and a full-beard offset chubby cheeks. He was barrel-chested like a boxer, and his grease-stained coveralls were in desperate need of a wash. Tucker mentally compared Enzo's body type to Leah's attacker. They could be the same man.

He got out of the truck and crossed the parking lot. "Enzo?"

"Who wants to know?"

He took a long drag on his cigarette, the picture of nonchalance, but Tucker didn't miss the stiffening of his shoulders or the sharp calculation in his gaze. This man was no one's fool. The best way to gain his cooperation was to play it straight.

"I'm Tucker." He gestured to his friend. "This is Nathan. We'd like to talk to you about Kaylee Ross."

Enzo's brows lifted slightly. "That girl's gone. Ain't nobody seen her in months."

"Rumor has it, you had an altercation with her before she left town. Something about dog fighting with your pit bull."

Enzo took another long drag and then slowly exhaled. Smoke wrapped around his head. The rain had petered out, but dark clouds hovering in the distance promised more thunderstorms on the way. Tucker could feel the electricity charging the air. Or maybe that was the silent aggression coming from Enzo. The mechanic narrowed his gaze. "You two cops?"

"Nope. I'm a friend of Kaylee's brother." Tucker kept his hands at his side, long and loose. The stance was designed to appear casual, but it left his hands free should trouble start. He had no intention of fighting Enzo. But the choice might not be his. A man like Enzo only respected those he considered equals. "Any truth to the rumor about your fight with Kaylee?"

Enzo drew up closer, into his space, and puffed out his chest. "You have a lotta nerve rolling up here and asking me questions. Who do you think you are, homeboy?"

"A man looking for the truth." Tucker met his gaze. He'd stared down men a lot worse than Enzo and lived to tell the tale. "I didn't come here for a fight, but trust me when I say, if you take a swing at me, I'll finish it. Now, back out of my space and let's deal with this like men."

"I'd listen to him if I were you." Nathan's voice was low but self-assured. "You're staring at an Army Ranger. That's special ops training, Enzo. He can smear the ground with you and not break a sweat."

A flicker of fear floated through the dark coldness in Enzo's eyes. Wise man. It was one thing to take on a street thug; it was quite another to mess with a military man. Even a former one.

Enzo backed out of Tucker's face with his hands up in the classic sign of surrender. "I ain't looking for a fight either. Had the cops breathing down my neck one too many times as it is."

Tucker let out the breath he was holding and tucked his thumbs into his jean pockets. "Did they question you about Kaylee's disappearance?"

"Naw, homeboy, I had nothing to do with that girl leaving town." He took a final drag of his cigarette before tossing it to the ground and stamping it with the heel of his steel-toe work boot. Enzo scratched his neck. "She bailed. Ran out with her boyfriend or something like that."

"Then you won't mind clearing the air." Tucker rocked back on his heels. "Listen, Enzo, if you don't answer our questions, the next stop we make is the Knoxville Police Department. The choice is yours. What happened between you and Kaylee at the vet clinic?"

The threat of police involvement seemed to convince Enzo to comply. He shrugged. "It wasn't anything. She accused me of using my pit bull for dog fighting. I told her she was crazy. That was it."

"I heard it got heated between you two."

He grinned, flashing cavity damaged teeth. "I've got a temper. Won't deny it. But so what? It don't mean anything."

Tucker didn't agree. Enzo was exactly the kind of guy who'd exact revenge for being slighted. A tattoo was hidden just under the collar of his shirt, visible for a brief moment when he scratched his neck. A gang symbol.

The Jackals operated in Austin for the most part, but since Knoxville was only an hour away, it wasn't inconceivable that they'd spread this way. They were ruthless. Had Kaylee gotten tangled up in something much bigger than she realized?

Tucker kept his gaze locked on the other man. "Are you involved in dog fighting?"

"Nope." He casually reached into his overall pockets and pulled out a pack of cigarettes. "That's illegal."

Enzo was lying. It was there in the flicker of his mouth. An uneasy feeling centered in the pit of Tucker's stomach. He could easily picture Enzo attacking Kaylee and being creepy enough to wear a pig mask while terrorizing Leah.

There was one problem. There hadn't been a flicker of recognition when Enzo first saw Tucker. He'd tangled with Leah's attacker on several occasions. The man had gotten a good look at his face. Was Enzo that skillful of an actor? Tucker didn't think so.

A man came out of the mechanic shop, stopped short when he saw the crowd at the corner of the building, and then hollered for Enzo to return to work. Enzo ignored him, igniting the end of another cigarette with a skull lighter before pinching it between two grimy fingers. "Listen, here's the deal. I had words with Kaylee, but from what I hear, that girl was messy. She made a lot of people mad."

"What do you mean?"

"She was always sticking her nose where it don't belong. It was better she left town, and if I were you, I would stop looking for her." His eyes turned snakelike. Cold and calculated. "If she ever shows her face in town again, she might find herself in trouble."

A chill crept over Tucker's skin despite the warm temperatures. "Where else did she stick her nose? I need specifics, Enzo."

"You ain't gonna get them from me. I don't snitch." He tucked a strand of hair behind his ear. "I gotta get back to work."

"Cory Olsen. Do you know him?"

He flashed a smile over his shoulder. "Yeah, homeboy, I know him. Careful with that one. Cory has friends in high places."

Enzo disappeared inside the shop in a cloud of smoke, like an evil magician. Nathan blew out a breath. "I don't know if there was a hidden message in his answer, or if I'm looking for things that aren't there."

"Same." Frustration clawed at Tucker. "Enzo has a gang tattoo. The Jackals."

"Yeah, I noticed it."

"Could Cory be working with them? Maybe supplying the gang with drugs?"

Nathan frowned. "I can't see that partnership going well. Besides, law enforcement believes the Jackals have their own drug trade going. If anything, Cory would be a rival." He twirled his car keys around on one finger. "Enzo is the kind who has eyes and ears everywhere. Maybe he's heard rumors that Cory is involved in Kaylee's disappearance. It could explain his cryptic behavior. Or, like I said, we're looking for something that isn't there."

"Yeah." Tucker glanced at the mechanic's shop. He had the urge to run inside and question Enzo more, but they wouldn't get any information from him. It was a lost cause. "Let's get out of here—"

His cell phone rang. Tucker removed it from his belt and his heart jumped at the sight of Leah's caller ID flashing across his screen. He pressed the accept button. "Are you okay?"

"I'm fine, but you need to pick me up ASAP. We got a new lead from the tip line."

SEVENTEEN

Leah clutched her umbrella as she maneuvered her way across the puddle-coated sidewalk. Galoshes protected her feet from the rain, but the downpour soaked the knees of her pants and occasionally pelted the side of her face. The wind kicked up, sending leaves and debris from nearby trash cans flying down the street.

Beside her, Tucker held his own umbrella, although it didn't cover his broad shoulders. His T-shirt was soaked, the fabric molding to the curves and indents of his muscles. Despite the seriousness of their errand, Leah had a hard time keeping her head around him. Memories of their heated kisses and his tender embrace floated through her mind. The man was a distraction.

Lightning bolted across the sky, followed by a boom of thunder. Tucker glanced at the storm clouds. "This weather is crazy. It wasn't even raining ten minutes ago."

"Haven't you heard the saying Texans use?" She nudged him with her elbow. "Don't like the weather? Give it a minute. It'll change."

He laughed. It was throaty and rich, reminding Leah of winter nights and starlight skies. She shook her head to clear the ridiculous notion. They weren't a couple. Heavens, they'd only started seriously talking three days ago. This was still the get-to-know-you stage. Yes, it'd been accelerated, thanks to the threats on her life. But still...no rational human being fell in love with someone over the course of a few days. It was better to focus on the task at hand.

Finding out what happened to Kaylee.

Another bolt of lightning streaked across the sky as Tucker yanked open the door to Moore's Hardware store. Leah ducked inside and closed her umbrella, keeping it on the large industrial entryway carpet to avoid dripping water on the tile floor. A sign requested patrons use thin plastic bags to cover their wet umbrellas. Leah tore one off for Tucker before taking one for herself.

Annoyingly, her glasses fogged. Leah tugged them off and dried them with the edge of her shirt before slipping them back on. The hardware store was empty of customers. Not a surprise, given the weather. Leah swiped her feet on the mat before beelining for the checkout counter. A woman was typing something on the computer behind the counter. Tall with dark hair and a pointy chin, she was the spitting image of her grandmother. Barely out of college, she wore a polo shirt with the store emblem on the front and slacks. Her name tag said Becky.

Becky Moore. Her grandparents owned the hardware store, although Leah didn't know Becky at all because her parents had left Knoxville when she was just a baby. Becky glanced up as Leah and Tucker approached.

"Hey there, folks." She smiled broadly, the effort bunching her cheeks and making creases along her eyes. "What can I help you with?"

Leah tucked a strand of damp hair behind her ear. "You're Becky Moore, right?" She waited for the other woman to nod. "It's nice to meet you. My name is Leah Gray. You called the tip line set up for Kaylee. The person who took the message said you had important information about her disappearance. I'm the person who rented the billboard and is running the tip line. Kaylee is one of my best friends."

Becky's happy expression melted as sympathy darkened her gaze. "I'm so sorry. I couldn't believe it when I saw the billboard earlier today." She checked her watch. "It's nearly closing time. Grandma holds dinner for me and I don't like to be late. Mind if I lock up while we talk?"

"Not at all." Leah would follow Becky to the ends of the earth to find out what she had to say.

"Let me start by saying, I didn't know Kaylee had disappeared until I spotted the billboard." Becky twisted a key on the register and double-checked to make sure the drawer was closed. She yanked the key free. "Otherwise, I would've reported what I saw months ago. I'm in college and come to Knoxville to work for my grandparents from time to time when I have a break."

"So you were in town when Kaylee disappeared?" Tucker asked.

She nodded. "I was at our warehouse."

"Where's your warehouse?"

"Over on Fifth and Main."

Leah mentally envisioned the block. It was down the street from the vet clinic where Kaylee worked. Her heart pounded in her chest. "Did you see Kaylee?"

"Yep. It was storming that night. Kinda like now. I spotted Kaylee walking up the road toward town and was thinking about hopping in my car to give her a lift, but before I could, another vehicle drove up. She spoke to the driver for a second or two and then hopped inside the car."

Leah shared a glance with Tucker. Whoever was in that vehicle, it had to have been someone Kaylee knew. She'd gotten into the car willingly. Leah followed Becky to a storage room. "Did you get a look at the driver?"

"Nope." Becky wheeled out a mop and bucket. "And I didn't pay attention to the license plate. Mind you, I didn't have any idea it would be important. But the car was distinctive. It was some kind of sedan, rusted and old looking. It was gray or maybe dark blue, but it had a gold driver's-side door. That's what I remember most. How wet and miserable Kaylee looked in the rain and that gold driver's-side door." She paused and blinked rapidly, as if holding back tears. "As women, we're told to be careful. My dad drilled it into my head before I went to college to be mindful of my surroundings. I'm not great about that all the time, especially in Knoxville. It always felt so safe here and now...I wish I'd known..."

Leah reached out and grasped the woman's arm. She gave it a gentle squeeze. "You've done more than you realize. Thank you so much for calling the tip line."

Becky gave her a watery smile. "Do you think you'll find her?"

"Yes. No one will stop me from getting to the truth."

Not even the man trying to kill her.

They spoke for a few more minutes with Becky, but it was clear she didn't have any more helpful information. They bid her goodbye and stepped back into the rain.

Tucker kept close to Leah's side, his gaze sharp as they crossed the street back to his truck. Once inside the vehicle, she re-cleaned her foggy glasses and then fumbled for her cell phone. "I'm going to call this in to Chief Garcia."

"Good idea." Tucker pulled out of the parking spot and steered the vehicle toward the country road leading to Leah's home.

She spent the next few minutes speaking with the police chief. He promised to follow up on the lead, which was the most she could ask for. When she hung up, Leah leaned against the headrest. "Well, we know Kaylee got into the car willingly. I don't recognize the vehicle Becky described though. Do you think it's the same one the attacker used to flee Nelson's Diner?"

"Could be. I didn't get a good look at the vehicle."

"Me neither. It was dark and everything happened so fast." Leah reached up and brushed her fingers along the cut near Tucker's hairline. "I was scared for you. It doesn't feel good to know you're in danger because of me."

"I'm not. I'm here because I want to protect you."

He took her hand and pressed it against his warm lips. A delicious shiver raced across her skin. The act was intimate and tender. It was something she could get used to.

Suddenly, the truck swerved. Leah screamed involuntarily as her seat dropped toward the road. Her head rapped against the window as her seat belt jerked her shoulder. Sparks flew outside her window. A flash of black bounced across the grassy divider and into the ditch. In the back of her mind, Leah realized it was the front passenger-side tire, but there was no time to voice her observation. A horn sounded behind them.

Her gaze shot to the sideview mirror.

An eighteen-wheeler was heading straight for them on a collision course.

EIGHTEEN

Tucker's heart leapt into his throat. The steering wheel vibrated violently in his hands as he struggled to bring his vehicle under control. A horn blast came from the eighteen-wheeler traveling on the road behind them. It was far too close. Pounding rain and slick roads made for poor visibility and an inability to stop quickly, something the driver had failed to take into account. If Tucker didn't get his vehicle under control, they were going to be smashed. A collision with an eighteen-wheeler at this speed—even with his truck—would be deadly.

He twisted his wheel attempting to ease onto the shoulder, but his remaining tires hydroplaned on a patch of asphalt. It went into a spin.

The world blurred into a series of trees, road, and the eighteen-wheeler hurtling straight for them. Leah's screams echoed in his ears. Tucker drowned them out as he struggled to turn into the spin. The truck's response was minimal, the lost front tire making it almost impossible to control their direction.

Adrenaline shot through his veins. "Hold on, Leah."

He gripped the steering wheel with white knuckles as they spun off the road. The left side of the vehicle smashed against a tree. Glass shattered, peppering Tucker with tiny pebbles. Another horn blasted through the air. The eighteen-wheeler blew past them before disappearing around the bend.

"Leah, are you okay?" Tucker peeled his hands from the steering wheel and turned toward her. A pain shot through the back of his neck, but he ignored it. Nothing mattered if Leah was hurt.

Her complexion was ashen and she appeared dazed, but there were no signs of obvious injury. She swallowed hard and blinked a few times. "I'm okay." She raised a shaky hand to her left temple. When she pulled it back, blood was smeared on the palm. "Oh. I hit my head when the tire fell off the car."

Worry spiked through Tucker. Head wounds could be dangerous. Deadly.

Tucker pressed the button to release his seat belt. Pieces of glass tumbled from his clothes as he shoved his truck door open. A first aid kit was nestled in the storage compartment in the rear of the extended cab. He grabbed it before hauling himself around to her side of the vehicle. Rain instantly soaked his hair and clothes. Dizziness washed over him, every muscle in his body aching from whiplash, but he smashed down his own pain and focused on the task at hand. Taking care of Leah.

He opened the passenger-side door. Fear crimped him as he got a clear look at Leah's wound, which had been hidden from his vantage point in the driver's seat. Blood ran down the left side of her face in a rapid river. It coated her hair and stained the collar of her shirt. A nasty gash streaked across her scalp, deep enough to require stitches.

Leah blinked again, as if she was struggling to keep her eyes open. "What happened?"

"We were in an accident." He popped open the first aid kit and snagged an emergency blanket. Leah looked like she was going into shock. The first priority was keeping her warm. He ripped open the plastic covering.

"The tire fell off." She leaned against the headrest. "Sabotaged."

"Yep." Anger fueled the word. Someone had loosened the lug nuts on his tire while they were interviewing Becky at the hardware store. A crude but effective way to cause an accident. Almost as horrific was the fact that the driver of the eighteen-wheeler hadn't stopped to render aid.

Leah grabbed his hand as he tried to cover her with the blanket. "I'm so sorry, Tucker. Your truck is destroyed."

Wasn't that just like her? The woman was bleeding from a head wound, heading into shock, and she was worried about his truck. Incredible. Tucker pushed the blanket up to her chin and wrapped it around her shoulders. "I don't care. Keep this over you."

"I'm sorry. I'm so sorry."

Her voice was filled with tears now and it shattered him. Tucker gripped her chin lightly with one hand and planted a kiss on her lips. "Stop apologizing. This isn't your fault, first of all. And second, I don't give a fig about my truck. I care about you and right now you're hurt." He released her, replacing the blanket on her shoulders. "Keep this on you, sweetheart. I'm going to call for help."

He grabbed his phone from his belt, but there wasn't a signal. Knoxville, like many rural towns, had weak or no cell service in some places. Unfortunately, this was one of them. He smothered another nasty thought about the driver of the eighteen-wheeler who hadn't stopped to render aid. That wouldn't help him right now.

Leah's eyes were closed, her complexion pale. Tucker tore open a package of gauze and pressed it to her cut. She was bleeding badly, but head wounds were notorious for that. He was more concerned with her going into shock. Or maybe she'd whacked her head harder than the injury indicated and there was something internal going on. The thought struck terror in his heart.

A flash of headlights appeared. Tucker breathed out a sigh of relief. "Someone's coming. I'm going to stop them." He reached for Leah's hand. Her skin was ice cold, the delicate bones fragile and limp. He forced her to hold the gauze on her wound. "Sweetheart, you need to stay awake. Hold this here. I'll be right back."

She murmured something in reply, but the words were slurred. A memory flashed in Tucker's mind, brilliant in detail and impossible to ignore. William, covered in blood, his grip on Tucker's shirt loosening as his words faded into nothingness right before his body shuddered with one last breath.

No. No. No.

Tucker shook Leah, panic fueling his voice. "Wake up, Leah! Keep your eyes open."

She complied, stiffening as awareness jolted her. Tucker released her shoulders, once again pressing her hand holding the gauze to the wound. "Keep this here and stay awake, do you understand?"

"Yes."

The word was stronger this time. Leah was tougher than anyone he'd ever met, but she was still human. Mortal. Tucker could lose her at any moment, and it triggered every one of his darkest fears. Loving someone and then losing them. Like his dad. Like William.

Although he'd prayed at dinner the other night, his relationship with God was fraught with tension. He couldn't quite bring himself to surrender completely. It was too much of a leap, too high a price to pay when things were so out of control. Prayer hadn't saved William. Would it save Leah now? Tucker didn't have faith that it would. And as much as Nathan and Leah had both assured him that God didn't hold grudges, a small secret part of Tucker wondered if that was really true.

The oncoming car's headlights drew closer. Tucker slipped and slid on the soaked grass as he raced to the road's edge. He was about to raise his hands and shout when a chilling thought stilled his movements. Could this be their attacker? Had he followed them from town to make sure Leah and Tucker were dead?

It was possible. Tucker glanced back at his truck. Leah was barely visible in the passenger seat through the curtain of rain separating them. They had no cell service, and she was badly hurt.

There was no choice. Tucker had to risk it.

He shouted and waved, stepping into the road as much as he dared to block the car's path. Headlights blinked in acknowledgement, and the vehicle slowed down. As it crept closer, Tucker's hand went to the small of his back. He wrapped his fingers around the grip of his gun, but kept it holstered. If this was a Good Samaritan, he didn't want to alarm them by pulling his weapon.

If it was their attacker, however, he was ready.

The vehicle pulled alongside Tucker on the road. An SUV. Despite the rain, the wheels and undercarriage were covered in mud. The passenger window rolled down, revealing Holt at the wheel. He was wearing scrubs, his hair damp and sticking to his scalp.

Holt squinted. "Tucker? What on earth are you doing out here in the rain?"

A flicker of hesitation stalled Tucker's tongue. Nathan suspected Holt's involvement in Kaylee's disappearance, but so far, they hadn't found any evidence the vet was lying. It was a risk, but yet again, Tucker reasoned he had no choice. "We had an accident. Leah's hurt. Can you drive us to the hospital?"

Holt's eyes widened in what seemed like genuine shock. "Of course."

Tucker raced back to his damaged truck. Leah's eyes were open but droopy. She held the gauze to her head. It was soaked in blood. Every second counted. Tucker's heart rate spiked as he undid her seat belt and took her into his arms. "Stay with me, Leah."

Holt had gotten out of his vehicle and was holding the back door of the SUV open. Tucker raced across the distance between them, Leah a slight weight in his arms. A prayer hovered on his lips, but he couldn't bring himself to put words to it. Instead, he focused his attention on sliding her into the back seat before climbing in and placing Leah's head in his lap. "Hurry, Holt."

To his credit, the vet rushed around to the driver's seat. He shoved the SUV into gear and pressed the gas. Holt glanced at Tucker in the rearview mirror. "There's a first aid kit in the pouch on the side of the seat. Use it." He focused back on the road. "What happened? Is this connected to the investigation into Kaylee's disappearance?"

Tucker fished out more gauze and a dry emergency blanket from the first aid kit. He covered Leah and tended to her wound. Her eyes were open but didn't focus on him. Still, she murmured his name.

"I'm right here, sweetheart. Stay awake." He moved aside a soaked curl from her forehead before glancing at Holt. "I think she's going into shock. Drive faster."

"I'm doing the best I can," he snapped back. "The roads are slick. We're no good to Leah if we get into another car accident."

He was right. The rain was thick, the SUV's windshield wipers unable to keep up with the deluge. Holt's knuckles were white as he gripped the steering wheel. Every second creeping by was torture. Pure torture.

"What happened?" Holt kept his focus on the road. "Is the accident connected to the investigation? Is Enzo behind this?"

"I don't know. We questioned him, but he claimed to be innocent. Which is probably true. Someone saw Kaylee get into a car on the night of her disappearance. A rusted sedan with a gold driver's side door. Whoever was driving had to be someone she knew because Kaylee got in the vehicle willingly." Tucker switched the blood-soaked gauze for a new one. Leah lifted a hand and wrapped her chilled fingers around his wrist. Good. She was hanging in there. "Holt, jack the heat to maximum."

The vet fiddled with the dial and then warm air began flooding the cabin. He glanced at them in the rearview. "Hospital is two minutes away."

He flipped on his blinkers, indicating to other drivers he was in distress and slowed for a stop sign, but then sailed through the intersection. "I don't know anyone who drives the type of car you're describing. Did you talk to Kaylee's friend Phillip Webb? He may know more."

Tucker pressed harder against Leah's wound, half listening to Holt, mostly focused on the woman in his arms. "Phillip? I don't know him."

"They dated for a while in high school, but then he left town and was gone for a long time. He recently moved back to take care of his sick grandmother. It was my understanding he and Kaylee were hanging out again."

Leah's eyelids drooped closed and her hold on Tucker's wrist loosened. He lightly shook her and then smacked her cheeks when she didn't respond. "Leah! Leah!"

Nothing.

"Holt, hurry! We're running out of time."

NINETEEN

Leah's eyes popped open as she gasped for breath and sat straight up in bed.

Jax whimpered and nudged her elbow before licking her chin. She placed a hand over her racing heart. A bad dream. That's all it'd been. She took a shuddering breath and patted her dog. Weak light filtered in through the closed blinds on her windows. A quick glance at the clock confirmed it was midafternoon. She'd been released from the hospital earlier this morning under doctor's orders to take rest. The knock to the head had resulted in a concussion and the cut had required ten stitches.

A headache pulsed along her temple, streaking down her neck. Leah tossed aside the covers, snagged her glasses from the bedside table, and stumbled into the bathroom to splash cold water on her face. She winced at her reflection. Dark circles marred the skin under her eyes and her complexion was ghostly pale. Leah gingerly ran a comb through her wild curls before brushing her teeth. She also took some over-the-counter painkillers.

Jax and Coconut were waiting at the bedroom door, ready to be let out after a long nap. They ran ahead of her down the hall. Leah's steps faltered as the living room came into view. Cassie, her long hair spilling over a cushion, had fallen asleep on the couch. Tucker was flat on the floor. His expression was softened, but not even sleep could remove all the rough edges of his features. He was dressed for action in cargo pants, a T-shirt, and combat boots.

A wave of warmth and tenderness washed over Leah. Cassie and Tucker had stayed with her the entire night at the hospital. Neither one had left her side for a minute. It touched her deeply to know how much they cared. She was a blessed woman.

Leah shooed the dogs from the room before they woke Tucker. Cassie had a blanket, but Tucker was uncovered. The man didn't even have a pillow. It was amazing he could sleep like that. She had some extra linen in the laundry room. But first, she'd let out the dogs. Otherwise, they'd smother Tucker's sleeping form with affectionate kisses.

She stepped into the kitchen to find Logan had already opened the back door to release the dogs into the yard. The former Air Force combat medic was tall with dark hair and an easy smile. Fresh coffee scented the air. A mug sat on the table alongside a laptop.

Logan shut the back door. "Hey, how are you feeling?"

"Headache but nothing too bad." She pointed to the laundry room. "I'm gonna snag a blanket and pillow for Tucker."

"Don't bother. We're used to roughing it." Logan winked and offered her a charming smile. "Besides, the minute you get close, he'll wake up. Leave him to sleep. He was wiped out by the time you guys got home."

It went against her natural instincts, but Leah sensed he was right. Tucker had been to war zones. Surely her living room floor was more comfortable than some of the places he'd slept in. He hadn't gotten any rest in the hospital. Every time Leah woke in the middle of the night, Tucker had been by her side. He'd offered her water, held her hand, and stood guard so she could sleep without fear.

Leah had never felt so cared for in her whole life.

"Mind if I take a look at your injury?" Logan asked, his voice cutting through her thoughts. "I want to check for any signs of infection and apply more antibiotic cream."

"Sure." Leah sat in a kitchen chair to give him better access to her wound. "I didn't have a chance to say anything earlier, but thank you for coming to the hospital. It was nice to have a friendly face in the emergency room. I was a bit freaked out when I came to."

Logan currently worked as a paramedic with Knoxville EMS, which enabled him to convince the doctor to stay with Leah while she was examined. His calm demeanor had been reassuring, although it hadn't stopped her from asking for Tucker several times. As much as she liked Logan, there wasn't anything more to their connection than friendship.

He pulled on a set of gloves. "I'm glad everyone is okay. It's not every day the front tire flies off." Logan gently parted her hair and probed the wound. "Tucker won't say it, because he's afraid of scaring you off, but he was a mess in the ER. I thought we were going to have to tranquilize him." He gave her another wink. "He cares a lot about you, Leah."

Her heart skipped a beat. "I care about him too."

Logan reached for the antibiotic cream. "I'm sensing a *but* at the end of that sentence."

"No. I just..." Leah sighed, sagging against the chair. "Tucker and I have known each other for a while, but we didn't really start talking until four days ago. Isn't it a bit crazy to feel so much for someone in such a short time period?" She blew out a breath. "My mom went through boyfriend after boyfriend when I was a kid. She fell in and out of love like other people change shoes. I don't want to be like her."

"Forgive me for saying this, but I don't think you could ever be like her. You're too serious and straitlaced." Logan paused, as if considering how his words could be taken. "I mean, don't get me wrong. You know how to have a good time, Leah, but you're careful. Measured is a good way to put it." He squeezed antibiotic cream on his gloved finger. "I don't think it's illogical for you to have serious feelings for Tucker. Think about it. You guys have been through more in the last four days than many people go through in a lifetime."

She inhaled as the truth of his words moved through her. Logan was right. She and Tucker had faced down danger together by respecting and supporting each other. Isn't that the true measure of a relationship? It was what Leah had always prayed for. A love who would stand by her and hold her hand during the storms life brought.

Leah had been so fixated on not being like her mom, she'd forgotten to let God guide her heart. He would take her on the right path. She just needed to be brave enough to listen.

Tucker appeared in the doorway of the kitchen. His hair was mussed from sleep, but his eyes were clear. He took in Logan caring for Leah's wound and a flicker of something akin to jealousy creased his features. "What's going on?"

"Just making sure everything is okay." Logan stepped away from Leah and removed one of his gloves. "The wound looks great. Nothing to be concerned about."

She murmured her thanks and stood. Three strides brought her to Tucker. She wrapped her arms around his waist and rested her head against his broad chest. He immediately responded, cocooning her in the warmth and strength of his embrace. His fingers tangled in her hair to touch the base of her neck. Leah barely heard Logan leave the room.

How long they stood there, she couldn't say. She breathed in the scent of Tucker's cologne and let it soothe the last edges of her raw nerves. He gently rubbed the sore muscles along the base of her neck. "Everything okay?"

"Much better now." She tilted her head back until she was looking Tucker in the face. A smile played on her lips. "Of course, there is one way to improve things even more."

She rose on her toes but only made it halfway there. Tucker closed the gap between them.

His kiss knocked the air from her lungs. It was tender and passionate. As if he was pouring all of his emotions into it. One arm kept her nestled against his strong body. Tucker's other hand cupped her face, his fingers sending a wave of heat through her.

In his arms, she wasn't a cancer survivor with scars. Or a woman damaged by her mother's poor choices. No, with Tucker, she was desired. Whole. Special.

The kiss ended, and Tucker rested his forehead against hers. He was breathless, and a little thrill went through her at the knowledge that she'd done that to him. Jax scratched at the back door, interrupting the moment. Leah reluctantly extracted herself from Tucker's arms to let the dogs in.

She gasped as Jax and Coconut sped past her, soaked and mud covered. The rain had left puddles in her yard and the dogs had obviously been having a wonderful time rolling around in them.

Leah snagged Jax's collar before he could bolt across the kitchen to greet Tucker. Coconut, however, was a lost cause. Not that Leah should have given it a moment's thought. Tucker bent down and scooped up the muddy pup into his arms. Coconut planted kisses on his chin, her soaked paws leaving marks on his T-shirt.

Tucker laughed. "You need a bath, Coco. You stink." His tone was warm with affection. He glanced at Leah. "Should I fire up the hose? Or do you bathe them in the bathtub?"

"Garage. I have a standing shower in there." She used it after returning home from work at the shelter. Stray or abandoned dogs sometimes had communicable diseases, and Leah didn't want to accidentally expose her pets. She tugged on Jax's collar. "Come on, boy. You're first."

His gaze turned despondent as she half-dragged him to the garage. Jax wasn't fond of baths. Tucker followed, still carrying Coconut. They sudsed up the dogs, joking and playing around.

Leah's headache was gone by the time they were finished and her stomach hurt from laughing so hard at Tucker's antics. He was completely soaked, and mud stained his shirt and pants, but he took it all in stride. He towel-dried Coconut and even planted a kiss on the top of her head before setting her down. She bolted after Jax to cuddle in his bed, which was their routine after a bath.

Leah wrapped an arm around Tucker's waist. "If I didn't know any better, I'd think you had a soft spot for Coconut."

"I do." Tucker brushed his lips against hers and grinned. "Jax and your cat aren't half bad either. Even the Chinchilla is growing on me." He wrinkled his nose. "The parrots, however, still hiss every time I walk by the cage."

She laughed. "They're slow to warm up to new people. They'll get used to you eventually." The questions plaguing her mind since last night came to the forefront. Leah had avoided asking them but couldn't put it off forever. "Was I hallucinating or did Holt drive us to the hospital last night?"

"No, you weren't hallucinating. We were fortunate Holt came along when he did." Tucker frowned. "He said something to me about Phillip Webb. Does that name ring a bell?"

"Yeah. He was Kaylee's boyfriend in high school for a while." She stiffened. Phillip had been the school rebel and bad boy. Leah had never liked him and never understood why Kaylee dated him. Their relationship had been toxic. "Why do you ask? What did Holt say?"

"He mentioned that Phillip may have information about Kaylee's disappearance because they were hanging out. If I remember correctly, Phillip moved home recently to take care of his grandmother."

"He's here? In Knoxville?" Shock rendered her ice cold. "Tucker, if Phillip is in town, he might not just have information about Kaylee's disappearance. He could've been the man driving the rusted car with the gold door."

TWENTY

Phillip Webb lived in a quiet neighborhood with older homes on large plots. Huge trees—a mix of pine and elm—shaded the front yard. The grass was bare in patches, a casualty of the unusual heat that had given way to thunderstorms. Tucker closed the door to Leah's SUV and let his gaze sweep over their immediate surroundings. A couple of kids rode their bikes down the street. Dark clouds hovered overhead, threatening more rain. Cardinals sang from a neighbor's oak tree.

Quiet. It was the type of neighborhood shown on postcards or in movies as the all-American experience. The kind that spoke of families, kids, dogs, and all the trappings that came with them. Several of the houses even had a white picket fence encircling the yard.

He circled the SUV and opened Leah's door for her. She gave him a brilliant smile and slipped her hand into his before sliding from her seat to the ground. The warmth that spread through his body at the simple touch couldn't be ignored. Tucker had never considered himself marriage material. Kids were a faint notion he hadn't given much thought to. But Leah made him question everything. He longed to keep her in his life for as long as possible. The complexity and depth of his feelings for her couldn't be put into words.

She made him want to reach for more. To be better.

Tucker had always prided himself on excellence. He'd poured his heart and soul into Army Ranger training. Hardship wasn't something he shied away from. Relationships, however, had always seemed more trouble than they were worth. Tucker had convinced himself he was too much like his old man, and any woman who initially showed interest would eventually leave. Just like his mother had.

But last night, while keeping watch over Leah in the hospital, Tucker remembered a passing comment Pops had made to him once. *If I'd put my faith in the good Lord, then my marriage might've had a fighting chance. As it was, without God's guidance, we struggled.*

Pops had become a Christian later in life, after his divorce. He'd been faithful until his death and had shared his beliefs with his only son. Those lessons had been reinforced by William during their friendship. And yet, Tucker had stubbornly held a part of himself back, even as he followed the suggestion to pray. He'd never truly surrendered.

If he wanted to be with Leah, if he wanted to be the type of man she deserved and needed, then maybe it was time Tucker looked inward and truly decided who he was.

Leah tilted her chin toward the front yard. "There's Phillip now."

Her words brought him back to the matter at hand. A man was crossing the grass, a shovel in one hand and a rose plant in the other. His basketball shorts were mud spattered and his worn tennis shoes filthy. The back of his T-shirt bore the logo for a local baseball team and matched the cap resting low on his brow. Tucker placed him mid-twenties. Fit. His body type matched the man from the attacks.

Tucker kept that thought at the forefront of his mind as he followed Leah up the driveway. She lifted a hand in greeting. "Hey, Phillip."

The other man turned and squinted before his face broke out into a grin. "Leah? Leah Gray, is that you?"

He abandoned the shovel and the rose bush to meet them on the walkway. He stopped short of giving Leah a hug, but opted for a fist bump instead. "Sorry, I've been doing yard work for the last few hours. It distresses Grandma to see her flower beds in disarray."

Leah cast him a sympathetic look. "I heard she's sick. I'm sorry."

"Thanks. She's a tough one. It's kidney trouble, but we caught it early and she's in such good health that the doctors are optimistic."

His gaze drifted to Tucker. Leah quickly introduced the two men, and they shook hands. Phillip's expression was open and friendly, his grip firm without being challenging. If he was the attacker, the man was an excellent actor. There was no flicker of recognition in his gaze when he saw Tucker.

The garage attached to the house stood open. A Cadillac and an SUV were parked inside. There was no sign of the rusted car with a gold door. It didn't mean much. Phillip could've parked it someplace else.

Phillip planted his hands on his hips. "What brings you to my neck of the woods?"

"I wanted to ask you about Kaylee," Leah said. "Someone mentioned that you two were dating at the time of her disappearance. The police haven't made any headway on her case, and I was hoping you might have some insight."

Sadness shadowed Phillip's eyes. "We weren't dating. Talking, yes. I wanted..." He stared off in the distance. "I'm gonna lay it all out there. I was in love with Kaylee. We reconnected after I moved back home. Both of us were in NA. I made some terrible choices in high school and in the years following, but hit rock bottom and decided to get my life in order. I got clean. Went back to school for my GED. Then Grandma got sick and I moved here to help her. Imagine my surprise when I showed up to my first NA meeting in Knoxville and in walked Kaylee."

"She struggled a lot after her brother was deployed."

He nodded. "That's what she said. Kaylee and I started hanging out together, and we discussed dating, but we both wanted to make sure the foundation of our relationship was friendship. Our romance in high school was rocky and I think Kaylee was skittish. Rightfully so. I wasn't a good guy back then and was happy to give her the space and time she needed to see I'd changed." Phillip frowned, creases forming along his mouth. "Then she left town. I thought it was weird but...When you say the police aren't making headway on the case, are you telling me you haven't heard from her, Leah?"

"No. No one has spoken to or seen Kaylee since the day she disappeared."

Phillip's complexion paled. The freckles across his nose stood out in stark relief. The man looked to be on the verge of fainting. Tucker gently pushed him into a lawn chair set up inside the open garage. "Breathe, man."

"She's missing? Actually missing?"

Leah took a chair across from him. Her expression was kind and sympathetic. "You didn't know?"

He removed his ball cap and then scraped a hand through his hair. "Gosh, this is going to sound terrible, but I wondered if...I thought maybe she'd relapsed. It happens. I figured that's why she was avoiding me. Kaylee knew I would encourage her to get back into rehab." His gaze searched Leah's. Desperation seeped from him. "What happened to her?"

Tucker had a difficult time imagining Phillip was faking his reaction. And his explanation of why he didn't consider her disappearance serious made sense. Drug users often relapsed several times before finally kicking the habit for good. It wasn't illogical to believe Kaylee had become another statistic. If not for the attacks on Leah, Tucker would be inclined to believe the same.

"We don't know," Leah explained. "She left work and started

walking home when someone in a rusted car with a gold driver's side door offered her a lift. Does that vehicle sound familiar to you?"

Phillip shook his head. "No." His knee jittered. "Have you looked into Cory Olsen? I'm sorry to tell you this, Leah, but he was the one providing Kaylee drugs. She'd turned him into the police. It took a lot of courage. She was scared of him."

Tucker's gut clenched. No matter which way they turned, Cory's name kept coming up. "Did he ever threaten her?"

"Once. Shortly after she stopped using, he cornered her as she was getting out of her car at her apartment. Cory threatened to kill her if she uttered a word to anyone about what he did on the side." Phillip swallowed hard. "He had a gun with him. Kaylee was really frightened. She thought he was going to shoot her on the spot."

That sounded like Cory. Tucker frowned. "The police investigated Cory. They couldn't find any evidence that he was dealing drugs."

Phillip snorted. "Cory's not a fool. I'm sure he was tipped off when Kaylee turned him into the police. Not much stays quiet in Knoxville."

"Do you think he would've hurt her after the fact?"

"Yeah. It sends a message to anyone else in town thinking of turning on him." Phillip's leg jittered faster. "Men like Cory take revenge."

That could explain why Cory was after Leah too. He considered the billboard and her continuous pleas to keep Kaylee's case alive to be a challenge.

On the other hand, the police had investigated Cory for the attacks against Leah and hadn't come up with any hard evidence. Was that because they were all focused on the wrong man? It was something to consider. After all, Kaylee had willingly gotten into the rusted vehicle with the gold door. It was hard to believe she would've done so if Cory had been behind the wheel.

Tucker rocked back on his heels. There was another suspect on their list, and while Holt had driven them to the hospital last night, Tucker wasn't entirely sure the vet could be trusted. "What was Kaylee's relationship like with her boss, Holt?"

Phillip started. His knee stopped moving. "Holt? Uh, it was fine, I think. He asked her out a few times, but Kaylee turned him down. She felt uncomfortable for a while after that and considered looking for another job."

"Uncomfortable how?"

"He watched her with customers. Brushed up against her while they were doing an exam. It wasn't anything overt, but it was consistent and it bothered her. Then things seemed to smooth out. Holt started dating another woman in town—I'm not sure who—and Kaylee was relieved. She finally felt like he'd lost interest in her."

Interesting. Phillip's observations matched Leah's. Tucker tucked that information in the back of his mind to ponder later. "Did Kaylee ever discuss the argument she had with a customer over his dog? She suspected he was using the animal for dog fighting."

"She did mention it in passing, but I remember her being more upset that Holt didn't back her up. That and she feared the animal was being abused. I know she reported the customer to Chief Garcia."

That confirmed the story Holt told them. "Can you think of anyone else who might want to hurt Kaylee?"

Phillip shook his head. "Other than Cory, no." Tears filmed the other man's eyes. "I should've talked to more people. I just assumed..."

"You couldn't have known." Tucker had intimate knowledge with the what-if game. He was still on the merry-go-round, and it was exhausting. "If you think of anything else, please call me."

He gave Phillip his phone number before escorting Leah back to her SUV. Once they were out of earshot, he asked, "What do you think?"

"I was wrong about Phillip. I don't think he's involved." She cast a glance over her shoulder at the man still sitting in the lawn chair. Phillip's head rested in his hands. "I mean...look at him. He's crushed. Phillip treated Kaylee badly in high school—he was always putting her down—but if he's received help and counseling since then..." She shrugged. "People change. Heaven knows, I'm not the same person I was in high school."

Neither was Tucker. He was inclined to agree with Leah's assessment, but he'd still do a thorough background check on Phillip. With the threats increasing, he wouldn't leave any stone unturned.

Leah's life depended on it.

TWENTY-ONE

Leah gripped her cell phone, listening to the ringing on the other end of the line. Every second the call went unanswered ramped up her anxiety and worry. She'd texted and called her mother numerous times since the attack at the diner. Mimi hadn't responded.

Two days. It'd been two days since she'd last spoken to her mother, and so much had happened since then. The car accident and hospital stay, for starters. The attacks were coming faster and getting more intense. Adding to her concern was the fact that Cory's name kept coming up. So far, several people had confirmed Cory was dealing drugs. What Leah couldn't wrap her brain around was why the authorities couldn't find any evidence of his illegal activity.

What did that mean for Mimi? Leah didn't know, but she was worried about her mom. She tossed the cell phone on her nightstand and reached for Coconut, who was pawing at her pant leg for attention. The little dog wriggled and kissed Leah's chin. It brought an instant smile to her face. Every problem was easier with puppy kisses. "You're a good girl, aren't you?"

Not one to be left out, Jax put a paw on Leah's leg. She kissed the Lab-mix between his sweet brown eyes. "I love you, too, Jaxie."

Her cell phone rang. Leah's heart skipped a beat. She scooped up the device, but her excitement quickly turned to dread when she spotted the number flashing across the screen. Dr. Jamie Francis. Her oncologist.

For half a heartbeat, Leah's finger hovered over the reject button. The threats on her life were stressful enough to deal with. Getting bad news from her doctor might send her into a tailspin of despair. But not answering brought its own set of problems. Leah would simply stew about it hour after hour, unable to forget her doctor had called.

She sent up a prayer for strength and hit the accept button. "Hello."

"Hi, Ms. Gray. This is Lucy from Dr. Francis's office. The doctor would like to set an appointment up to meet next week to discuss your test results. Does Monday morning at 10:30 work for you?"

Ice ran through Leah's veins. Her mouth went dry, and it took three times to find her voice. "That's fine." The words came out in a croak. "Excuse me, but is there a problem with my test results?"

"I don't have access to your records, Ms. Gray. I'm just the receptionist. The doctor will explain everything at your appointment."

Leah confirmed the date and time. Then she hung up the phone and tossed it back on the nightstand as if it was a snake ready to strike. Tears flooded her vision. Would the doctor want to meet if everything was okay? Panic and dread rolled over her like an approaching hurricane.

No. Leah took a deep breath and tried to quell her emotions. She wouldn't give into negative thoughts. One step at a time. Thinking too far into the future without knowing the facts wouldn't help. Her favorite Bible verse sprang into her head.

I can do all this through Him who gives me strength.

God would never leave her. He would help her through whatever came next, just as He'd always done.

Leah took another deep breath, swiped at the tears on her cheeks, and then grabbed her cell. She stuffed the device in her back pocket, unable to leave it behind in case Mimi called.

"Come on, guys." Leah opened her bedroom door. "Let's go see what we're gonna make for dinner."

The dogs responded by bounding down the hall toward the kitchen. Leah followed and then came up short. "Harriet? What are you doing here?"

The diner owner gave her a broad grin. It bunched her cheeks and made her eyes twinkle. "Thought you might like a home-cooked meal."

Spread across the kitchen island was an array of delicious food. Biscuits, meat loaf, and ribs soaked in barbecue sauce sat next to a variety of side dishes. Leah's mouth watered at the amazing smells. She hugged Harriet, overcome by the older woman's thoughtfulness and generosity. "Thank you."

"No need to thank me. Tucker's been keeping Nelson and I appraised of the situation. We've said a lot of prayers for y'all." Harriet pulled back and patted Leah's cheek. "I even brought your favorite apple pie for dessert. Now you'd better fix yourself a plate, because Tucker went to alert the guys. Once those boys get in here, I can't promise there will be a lick of food left."

Leah laughed, and then to her horror, fresh tears flooded her eyes. Harriet's smile melted into one of deep concern. "Oh, hon. I know. Everything's overwhelming right now."

Her kind words unleashed something inside Leah. Harriet had always been like a surrogate grandmother. Her wisdom was a true gift. Leah sniffed, letting all of her concerns pour out. "It's not just the threats. I haven't heard from my mom and I'm worried sick about her. My doctor's office just called, and they want me to come in to discuss my test results. I'm strong, Harriet. I have God to lean on. But sometimes..." She sucked in a shuddering breath. "What happens if I don't find Kaylee? I started this to help my friend, and it feels like everything is piling on me at once."

"You carry too much on your shoulders, Leah. You always have." Harriet rubbed her back. "Burdens are meant to be shared. With God, yes. The good Lord is always by our side. But He gives us friends and loved ones for a reason. We can't go through life alone."

Is that what she was doing? Trying to carry the burdens by herself? Leah accepted the paper towel Harriet handed her and swiped at her face. "I've been taking care of myself for a long time."

"Far too long. But there's no shame in asking for help."

The back door swung open and Tucker strolled in. He paused midstep, taking in the scene with one sweep of his intense gaze. "What's wrong?"

Leah turned away, heat creeping into her cheeks as embarrassment washed over her. Maybe Harriet had been right about her natural instincts to shoulder everything herself. Hadn't Cassie said almost the same thing a few days ago? Still, she swiped at her cheeks to dry them.

"Leah's having a rough moment, that's all." Harriet picked up her purse. "I'd better get back to the diner before Nelson decides I've run off to Bermuda for a much needed vacation. Y'all enjoy the food."

She left. Leah felt rather than heard Tucker come up behind her. He placed a hand between her shoulder blades. The touch unraveled something inside her. It was all too much. She turned, burying her face in his chest and started sobbing.

He didn't say a word. Tucker simply wrapped his arms around her and held her close. The embrace was a cocoon of safety and warmth. Her old survival instincts flared, followed by an urge to pull away. She resisted. Harriet and Cassie were both right. Leah tried to shoulder the burdens by herself, but that wasn't working well. God had put Tucker in her life. Not just as her protector, but as her friend. Before Leah could stop herself, she was pouring out every one of her worries and fears.

He listened. And when she was done, Tucker gently used the pads of his thumbs to wipe the tears on her cheeks. His eyes were pools of sympathy and understanding. "I know things are scary and you have every reason to be worried, but you aren't alone. We're going to get through this."

We? Was Tucker talking about her and him? Or was he referring to their shared group of friends? Leah couldn't bring herself to ask. It wasn't fair to Tucker. Their relationship—if they were even calling it that—was brand-new. If her cancer had returned, it would be absurd to think he'd stick around through chemo and doctors and hospital visits.

The back door opened again and voices filled the mud room. The guys were headed inside for food. Leah pulled out of Tucker's arms. She didn't want the others to see her like this. "I'd better wash my face."

She fled the kitchen and hurried into the bathroom. As expected, her complexion was blotchy and red. Exhaustion seeped into her muscles, the kind that came from crying a mountain of tears. But Leah couldn't avoid the kitchen forever. The guys had updates on their suspects. No matter what was going on in Leah's life, the search for Kaylee had to continue.

Leah splashed cold water on her face. Once composed, she headed back into the kitchen.

Rowdy voices spilled from the room. Tucker had been joined by Kyle, Jason, and Logan. The four men were making plates. Tucker caught sight of her and smiled. He jerked his chin toward the table. "I fixed you a plate already. Wanted to make sure you got some of this delicious food."

The gesture was thoughtful and just like Tucker. He'd make some woman very happy one day. Jealousy flared at the idea of him with someone else, but she forced it back down. Her heart was in serious danger around Tucker. She'd be wise to remember nothing was promised between them.

For the next forty-five minutes, they ate and chatted about everything but the case. It was a welcome change. Leah's muscles relaxed as the good food worked to satiate her hunger. Tucker and the guys joked and ribbed each other about everything. It warmed her heart to hear his laughter. She even got in a few teasing jokes of her own. He responded each time with a stunning smile that nearly knocked the breath from her body.

Jason leaned back in his chair and patted his stomach. The scar along his face morphed as he smiled. "Man, that was good. Harriet and Nelson never disappoint."

"Nope." Kyle wiped his mouth. "That pie is calling my name over there, but I think we should discuss business before dessert."

The air in the room shifted immediately as everyone grew serious.

Leah leaned forward. "Did you find out something new?"

"Nothing on Holt. I dug further into his background and came up empty-handed. Phillip was the same. He's been arrested a few times on drug possession, but there's nothing in his past to indicate he's violent or would kidnap Kaylee."

Leah nodded. Her suspicions about both men had been dampened, so she wasn't surprised by Kyle's revelations. Holt had driven them to the hospital the other night. If he wanted them dead, it was the perfect opportunity to make that happen. Similarly, Phillip's reaction when he found out Kaylee was actually missing had seemed genuine. She hadn't sensed any deception or weird vibes from him. Leah pushed away her empty plate. "What about Enzo Murray?"

"He has an alibi for the lake attack," Logan said. "He was at a bar with a dozen other people. He couldn't have been the man in the pig mask who tried to kill you."

"Cory is a different matter." Jason's expression darkened. "I finally got some people to open up, and they confirmed he's the man to buy drugs from. Cory hasn't been in the game for a while—he stopped dealing shortly before Kaylee disappeared—but rumor has it, he's about to start back up again."

Logan scraped a hand through his dark hair. "This doesn't make sense. Why haven't the police found any evidence of his crimes? They raided his house several times and have come up empty-handed."

"Maybe he stores the drugs someplace else," Tucker suggested. "We can't assume Cory is holding them at his house. He's smart. It doesn't seem wise to keep the drugs in a place where the police will find them easily." He drummed his fingers on the table. "If Cory is trying to get back into the business of selling drugs, then the attention on Kaylee's case puts him in the spotlight. Several people suggested he may have been the man to hurt her. Kaylee was scared of him. It puts Cory at the top of the suspect list."

"It's attention he doesn't want," Leah added. "Getting rid of me becomes essential. Once that happens, no one will be looking for Kaylee."

"Not anymore." Logan gestured around the table. "None of us will let this case go."

"Cory doesn't know that. Trust me, he doesn't understand loyalty. I'm sure Cory believes that getting rid of me will solve his problems—"

Leah's phone rang, cutting her off. She pulled it from her pocket and her heart skittered. "It's my mom." She answered. "Where are you? Are you okay?"

"No, I'm not okay." Mimi's voice was full of tears. "I need you, Leah. Cory flew into a rage and...I'm hurt pretty badly. He left, but I don't want to do this anymore. Can you pick me up?"

TWENTY-TWO

Tucker didn't like this.

He gripped the steering wheel with both hands, his foot pressing down on the gas pedal, pushing his vehicle over the speed limit as much as he dared. Leah sat in the passenger seat beside him. She worried her bottom lip with her teeth and clutched the door handle. Tucker would've preferred she stay at her home—especially since this could be a trap—but wild horses couldn't keep Leah from her mom. Their relationship was complicated, but Leah loved her mom very much.

Mimi needed her. Leah responded. End of story.

Truth be told, he admired Leah for her dedication. Her default was to put others first. It'd made the shared moment in the kitchen more poignant. This amazing woman trusted him enough to cry on his shoulder. It was an honor to be there for her. To support her. Tucker didn't view the task lightly.

The GPS indicated they were close and Tucker slowed down. He glanced in his rearview mirror. Jason and Logan were following them. Kyle had stayed behind to watch over Leah's house, just in case this was some kind of ruse to draw them away from there.

Too many unknowns. That was the problem with this entire case.

"There." Leah pointed to a rusted mailbox with a large dent on the side. A sign hung from it, the faded letters spelling out Olsen's Junkyard. "That's the property."

Tucker turned onto the dirt road. Craters the size of dinner plates littered the path. Many of the trees had been cut back, providing space for a car graveyard. Rusted vehicles of every shape and size littered the grass. Weeds grew from an old refrigerator. Washing machines rested haphazardly near a pine tree, as if tossed there by a giant.

The house came into view. It was one story with a broken lattice bottom covering the cinder blocks it rested on. The front porch listed to one side and several shingles were missing from the roof. In the fading light of dusk, the peeling siding was dark gray. It matched the clouds hovering in the distance. More rain was coming.

Before Tucker could shove the vehicle into Park, Leah opened her door and launched from the SUV. He called her name, but it was fruitless. She was halfway across the yard before he caught up to her. His gaze swept their immediate surroundings. No sign of Cory. But that didn't ease the tension in his muscles. He heard Jason's truck pull in behind them. At least he had backup if things went south.

Leah jogged up the broken porch steps in three strides and pounded on the door. "Mom! It's me! Open up."

A shuffling came from inside. Tucker grabbed Leah's arm and gently tugged her behind him before he reached for his weapon. A snick came from a lock and then the door creaked open. Tucker's heart sank to his shoes. Behind him, Leah gasped.

Mimi had been beaten. Badly. Both of her eyes were turning purple and a bruise bloomed on her cheek. She clutched a washcloth soaked in blood to her forearm. More blood spotted her blouse and jeans. Her hair was disheveled. Feet bare. She swayed in the doorway.

Tucker stepped forward, grabbing hold of the older woman before she fainted. "Logan! Get your first aid kit."

He lifted Mimi into his arms and carried her to the sagging couch in the living room. His boots crunched over objects littering the floor. The television was smashed. Papers and trash were flung from one end of the room to the other. It smelled like mold and whiskey.

Tucker set Mimi gently on the couch. "Where's Cory?"

"He left." Her face was smeared with mascara. She locked eyes with Leah and tears pooled. "I'm sorry, honey. I'm so sorry. I've made a real mess this time. Cory said he loved me, but...you were right about him. He's not good for me."

"No, he isn't." Leah shoved aside torn magazines and sat next to her mom. She gently took her bleeding arm and applied more pressure. "What happened?"

"He flew into a rage. I've never seen him like this before." Her chin trembled. "That detective came by to see him..."

"Detective Walsh?" Tucker asked, although he already knew the answer. Cory's house was outside the Knoxville city limits. The sheriff's department had jurisdiction here.

She nodded. "Yeah, that guy. I couldn't hear what they were discussing, but Cory came back inside and was piping mad. He started beating me and tearing the place apart." Fat tears rolled down her cheeks. "I thought he was going to kill me."

"Oh, Mom." Leah hugged her.

Tucker had more questions, but Mimi dissolved into sobs. She'd been through a traumatic experience and what happened next had to be handled with care. So he bit his tongue. But that didn't prevent his mind from turning over the new information. What on earth had Detective Walsh said to make Cory so angry?

Logan stepped inside, carrying his first aid kit. His dark-eyed gaze seemed to take in the destruction in one glance and then he beelined for Mimi. "Mrs. Olsen, my name is Logan Keller. I'm a paramedic and I'd like to look at the cut on your arm. Would that be all right?"

Mimi nodded. Tucker palmed his cell phone and lifted it slightly to indicate to Leah he was calling the police. Then he stepped out of the house onto the front porch. Technically, he should call the sheriff's department, but Tucker wasn't sure what to make of Mimi's statement. Why was Detective Walsh talking to Cory? Had he been conducting follow-up questions? Or was something more sinister going on?

The police had never proven Cory was a drug dealer. Was that because he'd been tipped off before the raid was conducted? It could explain a lot of things. Detective Walsh had never taken Kaylee's disappearance seriously. He'd repeatedly avoided linking the attacks on Leah to the case. And now he was here, alone, talking with Cory.

Tucker's thoughts were dark and he had no proof Detective Walsh was dirty, but he also wouldn't take chances. He dialed Chief Garcia's number and explained the situation. The chief promised to head their way immediately. Tucker thanked him and hung up.

Movement in the yard caught his attention. Jason was petting his dog, Connor, a concerned look creasing his face. The German shepherd whimpered.

Tucker headed their direction. "What's going on? Is Connor okay?"

"I'm not sure." Jason frowned. He stroked the dog's head. "What is it, boy? What's bothering you?"

Connor shifted on his front paws. The dog was definitely nervous or upset about something. His nose lifted slightly and then he whimpered again.

Jason's frown deepened. "It's like he smells something. There was one other time I saw him act like this and..." He inhaled sharply. "There was a dead body nearby."

Tucker's heart skittered. His gaze was drawn to the cars littering the yard. The waning sunlight picked up on a vehicle half concealed under some branches near the road. Something about it felt familiar. He pointed to it. "That car is the only one hidden.

See how those branches are covering it? I'm gonna take a closer look."

"We're coming." Jason snapped a leash onto Connor. The dog fell into step beside his master, but his gaze was sad and downtrodden.

Weeds and tall grasses clung to Tucker's cargo pants as he picked his way across the yard. Most of the vehicles were in various stages of deterioration. Hoods were opened as if the vehicles were being repaired by unseen hands. It was creepy. A shiver raced down Tucker's spine. As he drew closer to the car, the warning bell inside his head roared.

A gold driver's side door. Tucker shoved the biggest branches off the vehicle to reveal the rest. It was a four-door sedan, in a peeling silver with huge rust spots on the side panel and bumpers. The car matched the one Becky had described Kaylee getting into. A light coating of dust covered the windshield, but other than that, there was no sign the vehicle had been there long.

Jason shook his head. "It's the car, isn't it? The one Kaylee got in on the night she disappeared." He pointed to the smashed grass nearby. "Someone drove it here recently. The other cars have been here long enough for the grass to grow around them. Not this one."

"You're right." Tucker peered into the front seat. It was perfectly clean. Back seat too. He used the edge of his shirt to lift the door handle. Unlocked. The inside smelled of bleach. He gagged at the overwhelming odor. "Someone has wiped it down."

Connor whimpered. He slunk away from the car. The wind shifted and a new scent reached Tucker's nostrils. His gut clenched hard. That smell was familiar in the most horrifying way. A person never forgot the odor of death.

Jason met his gaze, his eyes dark and shadowed. "The trunk."

Tucker found the latch, and the trunk snicked open. With leaden steps, he circled the vehicle, snagging a stick along the way. He stuck the edge of the branch under the slightly raised lid of the trunk.

He paused. The scent was overwhelming. Connor whimpered again. Tucker couldn't blame the dog. He wanted to run away too. Tucker questioned the sanity of his next move. There was no going back once he opened this trunk. No way to unsee what he would see. It would haunt his days and appear in his nightmares, but he also couldn't bring himself to walk away. He owed it to Kaylee. To William. Dread twisted his stomach, threatening to make him sick.

Tucker breathed in through his nose and held it.

He slowly opened the trunk.

TWENTY-THREE

"The body you found inside the trunk isn't Kaylee."

Tucker stared at Chief Garcia dumbfounded. Beside him, Leah looked equally stunned. Her hair was pulled into a loose braid, but a few tendrils had snuck free. They floated around her face. The bruise on her cheek from the accident had faded to washed-out yellow and the cut hidden in her hairline was healing well. But there were shadows under her eyes, proof of restless nights and uneasy sleep.

It'd been two days since Tucker had found the rusted car with the gold door. The woman's body in the trunk had been too decomposed to identify. He shoved the horrible memory aside and focused on Chief Garcia. He was sitting behind his desk. Outside the closed door, visible through the glass walls of the office, police officers bustled around the station.

"Are you certain the woman in the truck wasn't Kaylee?" Tucker asked.

Leah reached across the distance between them and grasped his hand. He interlocked their fingers but didn't take his gaze from the chief.

"I'm positive." Chief Garcia leaned forward in his chair. The leather creaked. "We confirmed her identification through dental records. Her name was Sally Myers. Twenty-three." He pulled out a photograph from a file folder and placed it on the desk. "Either of you recognize her?"

Sally was a dark-haired beauty with a sunny smile. Freckles danced across her nose and she had a crooked front tooth. Tucker's chest constricted as the image of the young woman, so full of life in the picture, melded with the decomposed body in the trunk. Anger coursed through his veins. No one deserved to be killed and left like a pile of trash.

"She's not familiar to me." Leah studied the picture carefully. "Is she from Knoxville?"

"No. Sally moved here about four years ago from Austin. She worked as a clerk at the grocery store. One day, she didn't show up for her shift and her boss contacted me. I did a preliminary investigation. Sally's apartment was furnished by her landlord, and she'd cleared out her personal items. Her purse, clothes, a suitcase, and her cell phone were missing. As was her car."

"Let me guess." Tucker's jaw clenched. "A four-door sedan with a gold door."

The chief shook his head. "Not quite. A four-door silver sedan with large rust spots. The gold door is a change. That's why I didn't recognize the vehicle when Leah first told me about it." He tapped Sally's photograph. "She disappeared eighteen months ago. No one has seen or heard from her since then."

"How long has she been dead?"

"That's the interesting part. The coroner places her time of death about six months ago."

Horror filled Tucker. "Someone held Sally for a year before killing her?"

The chief grimaced. "That's the theory we're working on. It's hard to tell based on the condition of the body, but it looks like she was strangled to death and then put in the trunk."

"That doesn't make sense. From the height of the grass surrounding the vehicle, it hadn't been in that location for a year. Was it always on the property? Somewhere else, maybe?"

"It's possible. We conducted a search of Cory's property but didn't find any new evidence. There were several places where the grass had been stamped down, as if a car was there recently. Most of them were hidden in the woods."

Leah shook her head in disbelief. "Why would someone move the vehicle? Especially to a place that makes it easier to find?"

"It's too early to know yet." Chief Garcia frowned, the movement drawing deeper lines around his mouth. "Cory is still missing. We've got every officer in the state looking for him, but so far, they've come up empty-handed. Has Mimi said anything more about where he might hide out?"

"No. We've been over it a hundred times, but I think Cory kept my mom in the dark about his illegal activities. She admitted knowing he was dealing drugs but didn't know the extent of it." Leah's expression darkened. "She mentioned that Cory and Detective Walsh met several times over the last year. Mom doesn't know what they discussed, but she found it weird. Cory apparently isn't fond of cops."

A commotion came from the bullpen. Tucker released Leah's hand and rose from his chair. Detective Walsh stormed toward Chief Garcia's office. His expression was thunderous, tie swinging with the force of his steps. A receptionist hurried in his wake, panic on her face. She called out for him to stop, but he didn't heed her order.

The blinds on the office door shook as Detective Walsh shoved it open. He glared at the group of them. "What's going on here?"

Chief Garcia rose from his seat. He waved his receptionist away. Then his iron gaze landed on the detective and his tone turned steely. "Is there some reason, Detective Walsh, why you believe it's appropriate to burst into my office this way?"

He sniffed and looked down his narrow nose. "I fear your judgment is clouded. The sheriff's office is in charge of this investigation, and any witness questioning should include me." Disdain curled his lip. "You're overstepping, Chief Garcia."

The chief's gaze hardened, and his voice became dangerously quiet. "I haven't overstepped, Detective Walsh. I'm in charge of the Knoxville Police Department, and everything that happens within my jurisdiction is well within my purview to investigate. I shouldn't have to remind you of that fact."

The detective raised his hands in mock surrender. "No need for us to be enemies. I simply ask that we work together." He strutted over to the desk. "Actually, it's good we're all here. I have some questions I need answered."

Tucker wasn't about to take a seat with Detective Walsh in the room. The man would see it as a sign of weakness and attempt to tower over him. Instead, Tucker moved to stand behind Leah's chair and placed a hand on her shoulder. She jutted up her chin and met the detective's gaze. "We're happy to help with the investigation in any way we can."

"Are you? That's good." Detective Walsh perched on Chief Garcia's desk. His heated glare focused on Tucker. "There's a small problem with your statement, Mr. Colburn. The sheriff's department thoroughly searched Cory's property. Twice. None of my deputies located the rusted car with the gold door. Then low and behold, you find it within ten minutes of being on the property. How do you explain that?"

The meaning behind Detective Walsh's question was clear. He was accusing Tucker of planting the evidence. It was a ridiculous notion. Leah's mouth popped open, but Tucker squeezed her shoulder gently to stop her from talking. It was better if he defended himself.

"It's possible your deputies missed the car." Tucker kept his tone cool and unbothered. "It was hidden under some branches when I first saw it. The other possibility is that the vehicle wasn't there when you searched, but was moved onto the property afterward."

He raised a brow. "You've had a lot of interest in this case from the beginning."

"You mean, since Leah was attacked at the lake? Yes, absolutely."

"Even before then. You came to see me and asked about Kaylee. I remember we had a long talk."

This line of questioning was getting on Tucker's nerves. "What are you accusing me of, Detective Walsh?" Tucker pointed to Sally's photograph sitting on the Chief's desk. "When that woman went missing, I wasn't even in Knoxville. I was half a world away fighting for my country. My only interest in this case is finding out what happened to Kaylee." He drew in a breath. "And now, in getting justice for Sally."

Tucker wouldn't rest until her killer was caught.

"If I were you," he continued. "I'd put more energy and resources in finding Cory."

Detective Walsh smirked. "Trust me, we'll find him."

His cell phone rang and he strolled out to take the call. Tucker let out the breath he was holding. He waited until the office door was firmly shut before turning to the chief. "Something about that man isn't right. I'm sorry to say this, Chief Garcia, but is it possible Detective Walsh and Cory are working together?"

Chief Garcia ran a hand over his head, smoothing down the gray strands. He was quiet for a long moment. "I need you to trust that I'm doing everything in my power to solve this case."

Tucker rocked back on his heels. Of course, Chief Garcia would never openly admit he suspected a detective of being dirty. It wasn't professional. The coded message, however, was enough to confirm Tucker's suspicions. But how much could the chief do? He had a small police force and a lot of citizens to protect. Serious crimes—like murder—were handled by the sheriff's department. "Running this case is going to be difficult."

"I won't lie. We're understaffed and in need of new officers. It's difficult being a rural police department." Chief Garcia met his gaze.

"But I'll do everything in my power to get justice. I can promise you that."

"We know you will." Leah stood and shook his hand. "Thank you, Chief. If my mom thinks of any place Cory could be hiding, I'll pass along the information right away."

"Please do so. And be careful." His gaze drifted to Detective Walsh pacing the bullpen. "This is far from over. In fact, I fear things are just getting started."

TWENTY-FOUR

Chief Garcia's warning plagued Leah during the car ride home. She kept seeing Sally's face in her mind's eye, unable to shake the cold chill settling in her bones. Someone had murdered that poor woman. The same person had taken Kaylee and was trying to kill Leah. Her mind couldn't quite process it all.

Tucker was quiet. She sensed he was also mulling things over. They'd spent enough time together since the initial attack at the lake for Leah to understand Tucker was a deep thinker. He'd turn things round and round in his head until he was ready to talk about it. He called it brooding. She considered it wise.

Since their moment in the kitchen two days ago, he hadn't said anything about her doctor's visit. Leah hadn't brought it up either. With everything else going on, it was a relief to let that issue fall to the wayside. But there had been moments she'd caught Tucker watching her. He'd smile and make a joke. Or lightly kiss her lips. The move would dispel the silent tension Leah sensed brewing inside him. Yet she couldn't shake the notion that Tucker was wrestling with a decision. About them.

She didn't want to think about that either. They'd agreed to take the relationship a day at a time, and that's exactly what Leah was doing. If her heart wanted something different...well, too bad.

Tucker pulled the SUV into the driveway and killed the engine. Dusk had given way to twilight. The first stars were appearing in the sky under the watchful gaze of a full moon.

Leah exited the vehicle and took a deep breath. The air was scented with fresh-cut grass, pine, and roses heated by the summer sun. Inside the house, her mother was waiting. Mimi would want to know the status of the case. Leah couldn't bring herself to enter yet. Cowardly, maybe, but she couldn't bear to cause her mom pain.

She settled on the porch swing. Wordlessly, Tucker sat next to her, gently taking her hand in his. His thumb skated over her knuckle, sending delicious shivers through her skin. She leaned her head on his shoulder and took another deep breath. Thoughts tumbled through her mind, but there was only one observation she wanted to run by him. "Sally was kidnapped and held for a year before she was murdered. If the same man took Kaylee, it means she could be alive."

"Maybe." He let out a long breath. "The chief specifically mentioned he searched Cory's property, but came up empty-handed. It's difficult to believe he was able to get rid of all the evidence."

"He could be holding her someplace else." Leah stared up at the moon, silently wondering if her friend was seeing the same sight. Or was she in some dark hole, a prison some madman had built for her? Resolve stiffened her muscles. "We have to find her, Tucker. Before she's murdered."

She didn't want to consider that they might already be too late. Hope was essential when answers were few.

"I've already texted the guys." Tucker pushed the swing with his foot and the chain rattled. "Jason and Addison are inside with your mom. Logan is guarding the house. Everyone else is on their way over for an update. We're doing everything we can to find her." He squeezed her hand. "Trust me, no one wants Kaylee home safe and sound more than I do."

Leah believed that. "Do you think Cory is the killer?"

"I don't know. The way Detective Walsh has approached the investigation never felt right. Then there's Enzo. He said Cory has friends in high places. I can't sort out if that was a warning, or if he was trying to deflect attention away from himself. It feels like we're missing something." His voice was troubled. Tucker sighed. "I need to think about it some more."

They lapsed into a comfortable silence. Cicadas sang a tune as the evening wrapped itself around them. Leah wanted to take this stolen moment and bottle it up to keep forever. She lifted her chin to look Tucker in the face. "I've avoided reality long enough. We should get inside and talk to Mom."

"I know." He cupped her face, his gaze dropping to her mouth. "But not yet."

Tucker lowered his head and captured her lips. Leah's heart rate shot into the stratosphere. Her fingers threaded through the short hair at the nape of his neck. She drew him closer. His touch was exquisitely gentle and yet full of passion and promise. She wanted to drown in the emotions set loose by his kiss. Escape to a place where only they existed.

But that wasn't possible. Leah pulled back, her hand running along the soft beard covering his cheek. A delicious sensation swept across her palm.

Tucker leaned in and brushed her lips with his once more. Then he stood, tugging her along with him. "I could sit here and kiss you forever, but Logan's had enough of a show."

Heat crept across her cheeks as her gaze darted across her neighbors' yards. There was no sign of Logan. "Do you really think he saw us?" She lightly punched Tucker on the shoulder before he could respond. Of course, Logan had seen them. The man was military trained and used to staying in the shadows. "Why on earth did you kiss me like that then?"

He grinned. "Don't worry. Logan's discreet enough to give us our privacy without letting anyone get close." His smile widened. "He may demand an extra slice of pie to keep quiet about it though."

Leah laughed. "That I can do. Harriet dropped off several fresh pies this afternoon. If she keeps feeding me like this, I'm going to be a thousand pounds."

"Not a chance. You're stunning."

With those sweet words, Tucker opened the front door. A cacophony of barking greeted them as Jax and Coconut, joined by Connor, met them in the entryway. Leah and Tucker spent the next few minutes greeting the animals with pats and kisses.

Abby, Leah's cat, meandered by. She scooped her up and scratched the cat between the ears. "Did you finally come out of your hiding place? Are you finally comfortable with all these people in the house?"

The poor cat wasn't used to the parade of strangers running through Leah's house. She'd put herself in witness protection under the bed in the master bedroom for almost an entire week. Abby meowed. Leah smiled and stroked her head. She was rewarded with a rumbling purr.

As Leah entered the living room, her steps faltered. Jason and his wife Addison were in the side chairs. Mimi sat on the couch, a sweater in her hands and a duffel bag at her feet. The conversation between the three immediately halted. Leah lowered Abby to the floor, fresh trepidation coursing through her veins. "What's going on?"

Mimi nervously tucked a strand of hair behind her ear. "I'm leaving."

"You're what?"

Leah blinked at her mother incredulously. The last few days had been hard on Mimi, but how could she just take off? Didn't she care about finding out the truth? Hurt blossomed inside Leah. It was just like Mimi to abandon her once she got her feet back underneath her.

It was the same old pattern. Leah was exhausted by the merry-go-round.

Mimi darted a glance toward Addison, who rose from her chair. The redheaded beauty was dressed casually in jeans and a dark green blouse. She crossed the room, her expression concerned. "It's a good thing, Leah. Hear her out before you make any judgments."

Addison reached down and tugged on her husband's arm. "Come on. Let's give them a moment of privacy." She turned to Tucker. "You too. This is a mother-daughter conversation."

The group left the room, heading into the kitchen. Leah stood for a moment and wrangled her emotions under control before sinking into the armchair Jason had vacated. She mentally reminded herself to give grace. Her mother had been through a serious trauma. Her eyes were still bruised and swollen from Cory's beating. The cut on her arm hadn't required stitches, but it was painful enough to remain bandaged. "What's going on, Mom?"

Mimi licked her lips. "I'm checking myself into a wellness center. Addison helped me find one that specializes in abuse, trauma, and addiction. It's inpatient. I've already spoken with the psychologist that runs it and she's extremely nice." Tears filmed her eyes. "I've had enough, Leah. What happened with Cory is a wake-up call. I've been living on the edge for so long, I don't recognize myself anymore. God knows, I haven't been the mother you deserve. I'm ashamed and embarrassed. And I'm so, so sorry. Those words don't mean much, I know, but I'm going to work very hard to earn your trust. I hope one day you can forgive me for everything I've put you through."

Leah's own vision blurred. She'd prayed to God for a long time, asking Him to help her mom. It seemed those petitions were finally being answered. "I'm proud of you, Mom. All I've ever wanted was for you to be happy."

Mimi dissolved into sobs. Her shoulders shook with the force of them. Leah sat on the couch and the two women embraced. It was healing and emotional and everything Leah needed. Something inside her heart unfurled when her mom stroked her hair, as she'd often done when Leah was a child.

"You have been my biggest blessing. I'm proud of the woman you've become, Leah. What you're doing for Kaylee takes courage and fearlessness. You're the bravest person I know." Mimi pulled back and swiped at her cheeks. "I'm praying you'll find her. The program doesn't allow me to have phone calls for the first thirty days, but we can talk after that. I know this is the worst timing—"

"No, Mom. Don't worry about me." Leah smiled and dried her eyes with a tissue she pulled from a box on the coffee table. "I've got friends watching out for me. It's important you get the help you need."

"I love you, sweet girl."

"I love you, too, Mom."

Mimi hugged her again and then lifted her duffel bag. "Addison! Jason! I'm ready to go."

The couple came back into the living room. Tucker trailed behind them. From the look on his face, Leah surmised Addison explained what was going on. He gave Leah a side hug and then kept his arm around her waist as they followed her mom outside.

Jason took Mimi's bag and tossed it in the back of his truck. When he opened the vehicle's door, Connor hopped in. "Hope you don't mind riding with my dog, ma'am."

Mimi laughed. "Not at all."

She hugged Leah once more and then climbed in the back of the extended cab.

Addison hung back. Worry lurked in her eyes. "I hope you aren't upset with me. Your mom didn't want to say anything until she committed to going."

"No, I'm not mad at all." Leah hugged her friend tightly. Fresh tears stung her eyes. "Thank you so much, Addy. You don't know how much this means to me. Mom has talked about getting help before but has never taken the steps to do it. This is the first time I feel like she's on a healing path."

Addison hugged her back. Then she hopped into the front seat of the truck.

Leah waved as they pulled out of the driveway and followed the vehicle with her gaze until it turned at the end of the block. Tucker wrapped his arm around her waist again. She leaned into his touch. "I've cried more in the last week than I have in my whole life."

He kissed the top of her head. "I hope these are happy tears."

"They are..."

Leah squinted, lifting a hand to adjust her glasses, uncertainty flickering through her. A shadow moved in her neighbor's yard. Man-sized. For half a moment, the streetlight caught on his face and recognition blazed through her. She'd never met him, but Leah had seen his photograph. She inhaled sharply. "Enzo."

Tucker stiffened. "Where?"

He must've caught sight of the man because he pushed Leah toward the house as Logan rounded the corner and took off after Enzo.

Panic swelled in Leah's chest. She didn't want anyone to get hurt. "We can't let Logan go by himself."

Tucker didn't release her arm. His grip was firm but not bruising. "Logan knows what he's doing. My job is to protect you. Hurry, Leah. We don't know if Enzo is alone or what he's up to."

TWENTY-FIVE

Later that night, Tucker stood on the front porch. His gaze swept across the quiet neighborhood. In the distance, a dog barked. Leaves rustled on the pine tree and an owl took flight. Logan had chased after Enzo, but the man got away.

What was he doing so close to Leah's house? Spying? Looking for an opening to attack? The worries and concerns rolled through Tucker's brain like ice cubes tumbling into a glass.

The screen door creaked open. Nathan stepped onto the porch. "Jason and Addison made it to the wellness center safely with Leah's mom. No one followed them and there was no sign of trouble."

"Well, that's a relief." He glanced through the blinds into the living room. Leah was nestled on the couch, the dogs snuggled up against her. Cassie sat nearby. The women were in deep conversation. "Does Leah know?"

"I told her before coming out here."

Tucker nodded and leaned against the porch railing. "Where are we on Enzo?"

"The man's alibi checks out. He was at a bar on the night Leah was attacked at the lake. I spoke to several patrons who were with him and the bartender. Enzo arrived at four in the afternoon and didn't leave until close." Nathan tucked his hands into his pockets. "Why he was here, watching Leah's house, I can't explain. Maybe we ruffled his feathers more than we thought during our conversation."

Tucker grunted. "You think he was here because of me?"

"It's worth considering. You got into his face and challenged him. Someone like Enzo won't take that lightly."

Nathan could be right, but it didn't lessen the tension cramping Tucker's insides. He wouldn't be okay until the killer was in a prison cell. "Something about the attacks against Leah has been bothering me. The first one—at the lake—the assailant was determined to kill her. After that...it turned into something else. Later that night, at her house, I assumed he didn't go inside because of the security alarm. But maybe that's not the case. Maybe he was luring Leah outside so he could kidnap her."

"Why would he want to do that?"

"It's his MO. He kidnapped Sally and then Kaylee." Tucker let the idea take form. "At the diner, the attacker was definitely attempting to abduct Leah. If he'd wanted her dead, he could've simply shot her."

Nathan shrugged. "You're assuming the assailant knows how to use a gun. I know this is Texas and weapons are common, but not everyone feels comfortable with one."

"Then stab her. Or strangle her. It would've taken a few seconds to slit her throat." Tucker didn't like remembering how close he'd come to losing her that night. The stun gun had rendered him incapable of protecting her. One second more...

He purged the thought from his mind and focused back on his theory. "The attacker didn't do any of that." Tucker stared at Leah sitting on the couch. Her hair was loose, framing her gorgeous features. "Either we're dealing with two different men—one who wants Leah dead, the other who wants to possess her—or something happened at the lake."

"What do you mean, something happened?"

"She fought back. He took notice."

Nathan inhaled sharply. "She's a worthy opponent. A challenge."

The idea made Tucker nauseous, but he nodded. "Yes."

Nathan's expression darkened. "If you're right, we're dealing with a very sick individual. Men like this don't stop. I know. Cassie nearly died before her stalker was caught."

Tucker remembered. It'd been perilously close. He let out the breath he was holding. "How did you do it, man?" He gripped the railing even tighter. It was a wonder the wood didn't snap in his hands. "I didn't understand what you were going through before, but now I do. How did you keep your head on straight while Cassie's life was in danger?"

"God. And prayer." Nathan blew out a breath. "I won't lie and say it was easy, because it wasn't. You and I are used to walking into dangerous situations. We've trained for it. But it's a whole different matter when someone you love is at risk."

It was indeed. Tucker glanced at the moon. "William believed. Wholeheartedly. But his faith didn't save him."

"That's not true." Nathan's voice was low, but the sound carried across the distance between them. "William is with the Lord right now. He's at peace." His boots shifted over the porch planks. "His death wasn't your fault, Tucker."

"Then why does it feel that way?"

"Because you're hurting." Nathan put a hand on his shoulder. "God doesn't promise us a life without challenge or pain, but He swears to walk through it alongside us. He's reaching out to you. All you have to do is reach back. Give Him your grief and your heartache."

"I don't know how." Tucker swallowed hard. "After the accident, when Leah was hurt, I thought about praying for her. But I didn't believe God wanted to hear from me. I haven't been faithful. I've rejected prayer over and over again. Second-guessed God's wisdom."

He kept his gaze on the moon. "I have a hard time believing He would listen to me. I'm not worthy."

As the last sentence left his mouth, Tucker realized that was the crux of his fears. His mother's abandonment, Pop hiding his cancer diagnosis, William's death...all of it pointed to the same thing. Leah had told him days ago that he was special and Tucker desperately wanted to believe it. But in his darkest times—like when Leah was hurt in the accident—doubt kept him from reaching out to God.

"The Lord always listens." Nathan's voice was confident and sure. "You're His child, Tucker, and you're worthy because He made you. It doesn't matter what anyone else says. God loves you and that love is unending. Nothing will change that."

Nathan's words were the answer to a prayer Tucker hadn't realized he'd been asking. He'd be terrified to take a leap of faith, but nothing less would do. He had to give his whole heart to God. Half measures weren't working. "Thanks for the advice, Nathan."

"Anytime, brother." Nathan bounded down the porch steps. "I'm gonna do a perimeter check. Call if you need anything."

His friend disappeared around the corner of the house. The night wrapped its cloak around Tucker. He lifted his gaze once again to the moon and the stars. The idea of William, at home with the Lord and at peace, softened the ragged edges of his heartbreak. "God, I don't know why you took William to be with you, but I've been angry about it."

Tucker continued his prayer, listing out all his pain and sorrow. Every word lightened the weight bearing down on his shoulders. A peace unlike any he'd ever known washed through him. He leaned into the feeling. Surrendered. "I know You've been trying to reach me. It's been one step forward and two back for me. Sorry for being so stubborn. I promise to do better in the future."

And he would. Tucker didn't know what the next few days would bring, but he was ready to face it. He would never be alone.

Tucker bowed his head once more. "God, I ask for Your strength and wisdom. Help me protect Leah. Guide me to be the man she needs and deserves."

He loved her.

The thought jolted him, but the truth of it couldn't be denied. Somehow, during all the chaos of the last week, he'd fallen in love with Leah. Her gentle nature and genuine sweetness had brought joy to his life. He was better because of her. Their future was uncertain, but Tucker knew he wanted to be in her life forever. Would she have him? Did she feel the same way?

As if the questions had called her, the screen door behind him creaked open. "Tucker?"

He turned. She was bathed in the porch light, a T-shirt and yoga pants encasing her slender form. Leah held her cell phone clutched in one hand. Excitement brightened her eyes. "There's been another call to the tip line. We've got a new lead."

The Knoxville Park was thickly forested, with hiking and biking trails weaving through the five hundred plus acres. Many of the paths led to the lake. The same place Leah had been attacked the first time. Tucker gripped the handle of his mini-flashlight and tried to dispel the sense of dread washing over him. A cloud shifted across the night sky, casting the parking lot into shadows as the moon disappeared.

"I don't like this." Tucker kept his voice low. "At all. It feels like a trap."

He'd waffled back and forth about the wisdom of following this tip, but Leah had been determined from the start.

She took a step toward the trail on the right. "The answering service specifically mentioned the woman was terrified. She refused to contact the police and insisted on meeting us at the old railroad bridge. The last tip we received led us to the rusted car with the gold door. We have to take the risk. Kaylee's life could depend on it."

Leah wasn't wrong. It was entirely possible this was a legitimate tip. That the woman didn't want to call the police was a huge red flag in his mind. Was that because Detective Walsh was dirty? Did she have evidence of that? Finding out where Kaylee was being held—presuming she was still alive—was vital.

The weight of responsibility weighed heavily on Tucker's shoulders. "Leah, wait. There's something I need to tell you."

He quickly explained his theory about the attacks and the killer's motives. Not to scare her. No, it brought him physical pain to think of hurting Leah in any way. But she needed to know what they were potentially walking into. Her complexion paled, but determination tilted her chin.

"Right now, this is the best lead we have. I can't walk away, Tucker." She kissed him. It was only a brush of her lips against his, but it was filled with meaning. "But thank you for telling me what you think. Let's pray this lead is real and we find Kaylee."

"I'm already doing that. Let me go first, Leah."

He pulled his weapon as they stepped onto the tree-lined path. He glanced over his shoulder at the empty parking lot. Campers used the park often in the summer, but the designated sites were on the other side. "If this mysterious woman drove here, she didn't park her car in the lot. I'd feel a lot safer if more of the guys could work reconnaissance."

The caller had insisted on meeting in thirty minutes at the bridge. The time constraint didn't give Tucker time to coordinate a team response. As it was, only Nathan and Logan were available. They'd taken up different positions and were secretly closing in on the bridge.

Tucker adjusted the grip on his weapon. Sweat dripped down his back as he followed the trail.

A bush rustled. He whirled toward the sound as a rabbit burst from behind a tree and skirted across the path. Tucker let out the breath he was holding.

Leah placed a hand on her chest. "That got my heart rate up."

He nodded. "The old railroad bridge is a few feet ahead, if I remember correctly." The sound of the river was audible as it rushed and tumbled over rocks toward the lake. "I'm going to flip off my flashlight and we'll approach in the dark. Hold on to my belt so you don't trip over any roots. Stay close behind me."

She did as he instructed, wrapping her hand around the back of his belt. Tucker doused the flashlight, casting them into shadows. The thick tree foliage blocked the moonlight. He waited a few moments for his eyes to adjust before continuing on the path. Leah followed.

The scent of her lavender shampoo wafted toward him. It was a poignant reminder of the risk they were taking and everything Tucker could lose if this went wrong. His heart pounded against his rib cage. Embedded military training and an iron will kept his feet moving forward.

The trees parted, and the bridge appeared. Rusted railroad tracks that hadn't been used in almost fifty years ran across. Tucker had been here once before. Wooden signs, unreadable in the dark, warned individuals to cross at their own risk. This area of the river wasn't swimmable. Too rocky and dangerous.

He paused behind a large oak tree. It provided a clear visual of the bridge without exposing them to a potential shooter.

"Where is she?" Leah whispered. "The instructions were to meet in the center of the bridge."

Tucker's gaze swept the area. Movement from the other side of the bridge caught his attention. "There she is."

A shadow moved away from the trees and toward the bridge. It appeared to be a woman based on the slender form and short height. She was walking funny. As if favoring her right side. At one point, her hand reached out and grabbed the railing of the bridge.

Cautiously, Tucker moved away from the shelter of the tree. Leah mirrored his steps. The bridge was wooden and weathered by time.

Some boards creaked under his combat boots. He kept hold of his gun, but pointed the weapon toward the ground. His gaze swept their surroundings before landing on the woman clutching the railing.

He inhaled sharply. "Becky?"

The clerk from the hardware store swayed. Becky opened her mouth but couldn't manage to get a word out. She pitched forward and Tucker caught her a second before she crash-landed on the bridge. Warmth spread across his arm. A sinking feeling pitted his stomach.

He lowered Becky to the bridge and parted the sides of the rain jacket she was wearing. A blood stain bloomed across her abdomen. "She's been stabbed." He handed his gun to Leah and ripped off his shirt before pressing it against the wound. "Hold this here, Leah."

He took his gun back. Tucker's gaze never stopped sweeping the area. They were too exposed. "Who did this to you, Becky?"

She didn't answer. Leah looked up, frantic. "She's unconscious."

"We have to move—"

A brilliant white light came from underneath them followed by a horrific rumbling. The wooden planks vibrated against Tucker's shoes. His body realized what was happening before his mind could fully process it. Someone had blown up the concrete supports. The bridge was about to collapse. "Run, Leah! Run!"

She bolted. Tucker scooped Becky into his arms and followed.

TWENTY-SIX

Leah groaned.

Every muscle in her body ached. The scent of rancid smoke filled the air. She pried her eyes open, squinting to focus her blurry vision. She didn't have her glasses. Her hand stretched out, finding only grass. She frantically felt the area and her fingers tripped over familiar frames. Leah shoved them on and forced herself to turn over.

She gasped. The bridge was gone. Becky lay motionless at the edge, perilously close to falling over the ragged side and into the water. There was no sign of Tucker. Panic struck Leah's heart. "Tucker!"

No answer. Leah crawled over to Becky. Nausea threatened, but she battled it back as she felt for a pulse on the other woman's throat. A heartbeat threaded against her fingers. It was weak, but it was there.

She pulled the woman to a safe distance. Her knees shook. "Tucker!"

"Down here." His voice came from underneath her.

Leah scooted to the edge of the bridge, the rough edges of the wood scraping her skin. She blinked, almost unable to understand what her mind was seeing. Tucker dangled from an extended rail line. In the darkness beyond him, the water rushed and raged. One false move and he'd fall and be killed.

"Tucker! Hold on! I'll get a branch or something to pull you up."

"No, don't. Get out of here, Leah."

"I'm not leaving you behind."

Tucker flexed his muscles and lifted his body in a pull-up style move until his waist rested against the broken railing. "I can save myself. Get out of here, Leah." He gritted his teeth. "The killer is coming."

Gunshots erupted from the forest. Leah spun, unable to discern where they were coming from.

A dark shadow stepped out of the trees. Something whistled through the air and Leah's body stiffened as electricity seized her muscles.

The pain was white-hot and unbearable. She hit the hard-packed earth with a teeth-shattering jolt. Somewhere in the back of her mind, Leah realized she'd been assaulted with a stun gun. She had to move. To run. But her body wouldn't cooperate.

The shadowy figure moved toward Tucker.

No!

The scream echoed in her mind. Leah clutched the earth, desperate to rise to her feet. A glint of black in the grass caught her attention. Tucker's gun. She hadn't fired one since William had taken her to the range. He'd called her a natural.

She shoved against the ground. Her shaky limbs refused to hold her. She crashed back to the earth as the killer reached Tucker, who was balanced precariously on the extended railing. Her tough warrior grabbed the killer's foot. He was attempting to throw the man over the edge of the bridge. A tussle ensued, but Tucker was at a distinct disadvantage.

Leah forced her limbs to move again. This time, she crawled to the weapon. She whimpered as her hand closed over the grip. She attempted to take the safety off but couldn't get her fingers to move fast enough. Her gaze shot to Tucker.

Everything went into slow motion.

The killer reared his free foot back and slammed it against Tucker's head. He followed the move by crushing his hand. Leah screamed, her fingers finally releasing the safety. She raised the weapon, took aim, and fired.

The bullet hit the mark. The killer pitched forward, nearly tumbling over the edge of the bridge. He whirled.

Leah's muscles cramped again as a new wave of electricity coursed through her veins. The prongs to the stun gun were still in her. She'd stupidly forgotten to take them out in her haste to rescue Tucker. Blackness crowded the edges of her vision. The gun tumbled from her fingers.

She fell back to the earth. The last image she had was the killer standing over her.

Then everything went black.

Blissful coolness washed across her brow, easing the pain gripping her head. A tender hand gently shook her shoulder. "Leah, can you hear me? Wake up."

She didn't want to. Darkness beckoned with sweet relief from the pain smashing her head like a hammer, but something inside Leah refused to allow her to drift back into nothingness. That voice...that voice was terribly familiar.

She pried her eyes open. Kaylee's gaunt face hovered above her.

Shock reverberated through Leah and she recoiled before launching herself into a sitting position. Her vision swam, and she groaned. She slammed her eyes shut to stop her stomach from revolting. "Kaylee..."

"Sit still." Kaylee's command was followed by the sound of running water. "You've got a cut on your head. It bled quite a bit."

The head wound from the car accident. It must've reopened when she was attacked with the stun gun. Memories assaulted her senses. The bridge collapsing, Tucker hanging on the railing, firing the gun. And then...nothing. "How did I get here?"

A coolness brushed against Leah's brow again. A cloth soaked in water, designed to ease her headache. She cautiously opened her eyes and then grabbed Kaylee's wrist, halting her friend's ministrations. The nauseousness was fading, leaving fear in its wake as she took in her surroundings.

A bedroom. The walls were painted a faded yellow. Leah rested on a single bed and in the corner sat a dresser topped with snacks and bottles of water. A bathroom was several paces away, visible through the open doorway. The only light illuminating the space came from a floor lamp behind her. There were no windows.

Kaylee sat on the edge of the bed. Her hair was long, nearly down to her waist, and plaited into a braid. Her complexion was ghostly pale and she was thinner than Leah had ever seen her. A bruise bloomed on her bare arm and another on her leg. She wore a pale shift dress that hung on her narrow frame.

Leah couldn't believe her eyes. Kaylee was alive. She'd hoped and prayed for it, but seeing her in real life was overwhelming.

Tears flooded Leah's vision. "I've been searching for you." She embraced her friend, horrified by the feel of Kaylee's spine under her palm. Every ridge and indention was apparent. But Kaylee was alive. There was hope. "Thank you, God."

Kaylee pulled back, wetness glittering on her cheeks. "This is all my fault. I'm so sorry, Leah. You should have stopped searching for me." She grabbed her hands. "He's going to kill you."

"Who—"

The sound of a key twisting in a lock cut her off. The bedroom door swung open, creaking on the hinges. Leah inhaled sharply, smothering a gasp.

Holt Adler.

A thousand questions ran through Leah's mind, but she didn't utter one of them. Holt's glare could've melted the skin from a person's face. He marched into the room, face mottled with fury. Blood stained the sleeve of his shirt. It dripped down his arm and onto the carpet. "About time you woke up, you stupid woman. You shot me!"

Kaylee shrank back. Leah couldn't bear to think about her close friend being left alone with this madman for months and months. What had he put her through? The bruises were proof enough of the indignities and injustices Kaylee had suffered. Leah was tempted to fly across the room and attack Holt with her bare hands, but wisdom held her in place.

"You attacked me." She forced herself to look him in the eye, remembering Tucker's theory about the case. Holt wanted her because she was a challenge. "I was protecting myself."

She desperately wanted to know if Holt had sent Tucker over the edge of the bridge into the raging river, but sensed he would use that particular weakness against her.

Please, God, let Tucker be alive.

The thought of losing him made her throat clog with emotion. Her hero. Her protector. Tucker had stood beside her through every pitfall without wavering. He'd supported her with encouraging words, let her cry on his shoulder, and listened to her confidences. Their time together hadn't been long, but every moment had been precious. Tucker had to be alive. He just had to be.

She loved him.

Leah wanted the opportunity to tell him. But first, she needed to survive this.

Holt took another step into the room and Kaylee cowed even more. He didn't even notice. His sole focus was on Leah. Hatred and anger pulsed off him. When he raised his hand, Leah braced herself for the slap.

It wasn't enough. His palm smacked her skin, the force behind it enough to drive her off the bed and onto the floor. Holt kicked her in the stomach and she curled into a fetal position. Pain radiated outward into every limb. Leah retched. She lost control of her stomach, tears blurring her vision. She'd never felt so vulnerable and helpless, not even in the throes of her chemo treatments.

A scream reached her ears. Kaylee launched herself from the bed and pounded on Holt with her fists. "Stop hurting her. Stop it!"

Holt flung her away as if she was nothing more than a rag doll. Kaylee smashed into the wall and slid down, landing in a heap on the carpet.

Leah wheezed, drawing air into her lungs, and struggled to her feet. It hurt to breathe. It hurt to move. But she didn't have a choice. She drew on her own inner strength. A gift from the Lord that had seen her through childhood heartbreak, a cancer diagnosis, losing William, and the kidnapping of her friend.

She wouldn't stop fighting. Not for a moment.

Holt spun to face her. "I don't relish punishing you, Leah." His expression was apologetic, but it didn't quite erase the gleam of satisfaction from his eyes. "You have to speak to me respectfully. You don't understand that yet, but you will."

This time when he stepped closer to her, there was no rage. He reached out to touch her hair, and she retreated. The back of her knees hit the bed, forcing her to stop. Holt stroked her curls, and she winced in disgust. The scent of his sweat and blood filled her nose. She was going to throw up again.

He didn't seem to notice her withdrawal. His gaze was far away and dreamy. "It's not your fault. Women like you have been told that you're equal to men. You don't understand the world order."

Suddenly, his grip tightened as his focus snapped to her face. He twisted her neck painfully. "But you will learn. I'll teach you. First,

LYNN SHANNON

though, you're going to sew up my bullet wound. I know you can do it because of your work at the shelter."

She didn't cry out despite the white-hot pain running down her spine. She wouldn't give him the satisfaction.

Holt tossed her to the bed, and she bounced on the thin mattress.

The door to the bedroom was still open. This was her chance. Maybe her only one. Before Holt could realize what she was doing, Leah reared both feet back and then slammed them into his groin.

Holt screamed and dropped to the ground. Tears streamed down his face as it turned fire engine red.

Leah didn't hesitate for a moment. She raced across the room to Kaylee, who was struggling to her feet. It was clear months of being locked up had sapped all her energy. Leah wrapped an arm around Kaylee's thin waist and steered her from the room. "Come on. We've got to get out of here."

They went into the hallway. Leah paused long enough to close the bedroom door and latched the lock. It wouldn't hold Holt forever, but it would slow him down. Then she helped Kaylee down the stairs. Her friend panted on the landing.

A door opened below them. Leah froze.

"Who's that?" she whispered to Kaylee.

"I don't know." Her eyes mirrored Leah's panic. "Holt's the only person I've seen. I've never been outside the bedroom."

Did the person in the kitchen know Holt had Kaylee upstairs? Or was it simply a good friend who didn't know about Holt's true nature? Leah weighed her options. None were great if the individual in the kitchen was Holt's partner in crime.

She peeked over the railing. The front door was underneath them. Leah had a vague recollection that Holt's house was on the outskirts of the county. That must be where they were. If she and Kaylee could get out of the house, they could hide in the woods and slowly make their way to the nearby highway.

Kaylee trembled. Fear clutched Leah's heart. Her friend was

weak and in no condition to make a trek through the forest. Holt's injuries wouldn't keep him down for long. Then he'd be hunting them. Perhaps with help from the person in the kitchen. For half a breath, she debated the wisdom of their escape. But what choice did they have? Holt would kill them no matter what. They had to try.

"Give us strength, Lord," Leah whispered.

"Amen." Kaylee smiled, even as fear and worry clouded her eyes. "Let's go, Leah."

They crept down the staircase. Movement in the kitchen indicated the mysterious person was rummaging inside the fridge for food. The sound of a soda being opened carried across the entryway. Leah's pulse pounded in her ears, so loud she was sure everyone in the house could hear it. Her shoes were silent against the tile floor. On tiptoes, she approached the front door. Kaylee followed.

Leah grasped the handle.

"Hey!" a man shouted behind them.

Her heart rocketed into her throat, but she didn't pause. Leah twisted the knob and flung the front door open. She screamed as a man loomed large, peeling out of the shadows of the porch in full tactical gear. Leah grabbed Kaylee, shoving her friend behind her in a desperate attempt to protect her. The man pushed both women to the side and lifted his weapon.

Gunshots erupted.

TWENTY-SEVEN

Tucker stared out the window of his hospital room. The view overlooked a nearby park. Kids played on the swing sets while parents gathered on park benches and picnic tables. One couple had spread a blanket on the grass and were reading a book together. It made him think of his future and what that entailed now that the threat against Leah had been resolved and Kaylee was found.

A knock came on the doorframe. Tucker turned, his breath catching when he caught sight of the woman in his doorway. Leah wore a pair of hip-hugging jeans and a blouse that played with the highlights of caramel in her hair. His heart picked up speed with every step she made across the room.

"I brought a surprise for you." Her smile widened, the chocolate-brown eyes behind her glasses sparkling with happiness and mischief.

Tucker brushed his lips against hers and grinned back. "What kind of surprise?"

Leah reached into her oversized purse and pulled out Coconut. The little dog yipped with excitement when her gaze landed on Tucker. He scooped the pup into his arms and kissed her head. She wriggled, her tail going a mile a minute as she returned his affection with kisses on his chin.

He laughed. "I'm pretty sure dogs aren't allowed in the hospital." Tucker arched his brows. "Something tells me you got this idea from Kyle."

The former Army specialist had rescued a kitten from a trash can outside the VA hospital. He subsequently snuck her inside his room, where she lived for several days before Kyle was discharged. Ms. Whiskers was one of the most spoiled cats Tucker had ever seen. Kyle adored her.

Leah lifted a finger to her lips. "I've been sworn to secrecy."

They both laughed. A knock came on the doorframe. Tucker instinctively hid Coconut behind his back, but stopped once he realized Chief Garcia was standing in the doorway. "Come on in, sir."

The chief removed his cowboy hat and entered the room. Dark circles and bags marred the skin under his eyes and his steps were slow with exhaustion. He offered them a weary smile. "I was on my way home to catch some rest after working the case all night, but thought I'd stop in to give y'all an update. You certainly deserve it."

He reached out to scratch Coconut behind the ears and asked, "How are you feeling, Tucker?"

"Almost normal." The tussle with Holt at the bridge had left him with a concussion and several broken fingers, but Tucker would make a full recovery. "They're preparing my discharge paperwork as we speak."

"Good." Chief Garcia stepped back and perched on the edge of the bed. "Well, Holt Alder has been arrested and charged with three counts of kidnapping, one count of murder, and two counts of attempted murder. That's only the beginning. The District Attorney is planning on throwing every charge possible in there. Holt won't ever see the outside of a prison again." The chief turned to Leah. "I hope that brings you some measure of comfort."

"It does." She glanced at Tucker. "What he did to us was bad, but it's nothing compared to what Kaylee went through. And poor Sally."

Chief Garcia's expression darkened. "According to Holt, he killed Sally by accident in a fit of rage. He didn't know what to do. Sally's vehicle was hidden on his property, so he put her body in the trunk. He'd already kidnapped Kaylee and was holding her in a separate room. When you pushed the sheriff's department hard to investigate the disappearance, Holt took notice. The billboard must've been the final straw. He initially decided to get rid of you. Then, it seems, his plans changed. He wanted to keep you as a replacement for Sally."

"Why didn't he kidnap me after the car accident?"

"He'd intended to, but wasn't sure if Tucker had already called 911. He decided helping you would get him off the suspect list."

It had nearly worked. Tucker wrapped his arm around Leah. Last night, she told him about sneaking down the stairs and hearing someone in the kitchen. It'd been Enzo Murray. He'd been shot and killed by the tactical force team that entered the house to rescue the women. "How does Enzo fit into all of this?"

"Holt and Enzo are second cousins. When his attacks didn't work, Holt became desperate. He enlisted his cousin's help."

"Hold on," Leah interjected. "If Enzo and Holt were working together, then why did Holt tell us about the fight Kaylee and Enzo had?"

"My guess is he figured you'd hear about it from someone eventually."

Tucker nodded. "Makes sense. Holt was also the one who led us to Phillip. He had us spinning our wheels, working to track down other suspects so we wouldn't look too closely at him."

"Exactly." The chief frowned. "Enzo knew Detective Walsh and Cory were trafficking drugs. He told Holt. They made a plan to frame Cory and then blackmail Detective Walsh. It solved multiple problems. Holt needed someone to take the fall for Kaylee's disappearance and Enzo wanted the men out of the drug business because his gang was posed to take over. He also liked the idea of having someone on the inside at the sheriff's office."

Anger flared in the chief's eyes. "Holt lured Cory to his house and locked him the basement. He planted the car with Sally's body at Cory's house. Once Kaylee was dead, they planned on leaving her body with Cory and making his death look like a suicide. Once it was all done, Enzo would begin blackmailing Detective Walsh."

"That explains why Detective Walsh was incensed when we discovered the car on Cory's property. They were working together, just not in the way we thought."

Chief Garcia nodded. "Detective Walsh told Cory earlier in the day that things were heating up and they couldn't get back into the drug trade right away. Cory was incensed. He flew into a rage and then took off. Sometime after that is when Holt lured him to his house. Once Cory was captured, Holt kidnapped Becky to use her to lure you guys to the bridge."

"Becky saw Kaylee get into the car," Leah surmised. "Holt must've worried she'd figure out who the driver was. He needed to tie up loose ends."

"Yes. Thankfully, she'll make a full recovery."

"And Detective Walsh?" Tucker asked.

His mouth flattened. "He's been arrested. Once Walsh realized the amount of trouble he was in, the man sang like a canary. We're taking down the entire drug-trafficking ring. Cory and Walsh will spend the rest of their lives in prison."

Leah breathed out. "That's a relief."

Chief Garcia twisted his hat in his hands. "I've apologized to Kaylee, and I'm going to say it to you both as well. I'm very sorry. A law enforcement officer is a trusted individual and what Walsh did casts a shadow on all of us."

"No, it doesn't." Leah's tone was firm and authoritative. "I owe you a huge debt of gratitude. You always took my concerns about Kaylee's disappearance seriously, and I know you did everything within your power to solve her case. I couldn't be more proud of the Knoxville Police Department. You guys saved my life. And Kaylee's too."

The chief's shoulders straightened. "Thank you for those kind words, Leah. Although I can't take all the credit. Without Tucker's help, we wouldn't have known who'd taken you and Kaylee." He shot Tucker a look. "Although I nearly had to arrest Tucker to keep him from raiding the house himself."

It was true. During the attack on the bridge, Tucker had an up close look at the assailant's tennis shoes and recognized the stains and tears immediately. Holt had been wearing the same ones at the vet's office and again when he visited Leah's house.

Tucker heaved himself onto the bridge just as Logan and Nathan came running out of the woods. They helped pull him to safety and called Chief Garcia to relay the information. Then they raced to Holt's house just as the state tactical team was mobilizing. It'd taken a lot of convincing to keep Tucker from entering the house on his own. Only the fear of making things worse for Leah held him back.

The chief rose from the bed and placed his hat on his head. "How's Kaylee doing this morning, Leah?"

"She's good. It'll take a while to heal, but I think she's going to be just fine." Leah squeezed Tucker's waist. "Phillip, her old boyfriend, is sitting with her now. He hasn't left her side since she was found, and I think his presence is giving her a lot of comfort."

"Good. If there's anything I can do to help, let me know." He stifled a yawn. "I'd best get this old body to bed before I lay down right here and conk out."

Tucker hesitated and then said, "One second, chief. I have a question. You mentioned being short-staffed the other day. If I was interested in joining the police force, would that be something you'd be open to?"

Chief Garcia's eyes lit up. "Absolutely, son. Come to my office next week and we'll discuss the logistics. You'll need to attend training courses, but given your military history, they'll be a breeze."

"I'm taking college classes to obtain my bachelors—"

"Don't worry about that. We'll work around your classes. I always encourage my officers to better themselves through education and training." The chief offered his hand. "You'd be a great addition to the team, Tucker."

He shook the older man's hand, pride brimming inside him. Chief Garcia had proven himself to be a man of integrity and his opinion mattered. It would be an honor to work for him. "Thank you, sir."

Chief Garcia shook Leah's hand, and she surprised him with a hug. He embraced her back. Then he gave one last wave and left the room.

Leah turned toward Tucker, her brows arched slightly. "A police officer, huh?"

"Yep. Being in the military gave me a sense of purpose and meaning. Since leaving, I've had a hard time. While searching for Kaylee, I realized how much of a difference I could make by joining the police department."

"I'm so proud of you." Leah wrapped her arms around his waist, careful not to crush Coconut or hurt Tucker's broken fingers. She grinned. "You're going to look very handsome in the uniform."

He chuckled and then bent to capture her lips in a kiss. His heart thundered as she melted against him. Coconut joined them by kissing their chins. They broke away laughing. Tucker patted the small dog. "Yes, we love you too."

He met Leah's gaze. His pulse quickened again, this time for an entirely different reason. Tucker reached into his pants pocket and produced a jewelry box. "I have a surprise for you too." He couldn't open the box himself, thanks to the broken fingers, so he handed it to her. "Open it."

She did, revealing a sparkling diamond ring. It'd taken a bit of work to purchase it last night. Nathan had driven to the jewelry store, and they'd done it over video chat. Tucker wished he wasn't asking Leah to marry him in a hospital room. She deserved candlelight and romance, but time wouldn't allow it.

Leah's eyes widened with shock. "What?" She jutted the box back toward him. "No, Tucker, don't. My appointment with the oncologist is in an hour. Now's not the time—"

"Now is the perfect time." Tucker got down on one knee. "Leah Marie Gray, I have fallen head over heels in love with you. This week has taught me that there's nothing you and I can't face together. Whatever our future holds, I want to spend it with you. Please..." A lump formed in his throat, and it took Tucker several tries to shove it down. "Please make me the happiest man in the world and agree to be my wife. Will you marry me, Leah?"

Tears dropped from her eyes onto her cheeks. "Yes. Yes, I'll marry you."

Tucker whooped and rose, capturing her lips for another kiss. It was full of passion and promise. He'd found the love of his life. Every moment with her was a precious gift, and Tucker thanked God again and again for the blessing.

TWENTY-EIGHT

Six months later

Leah adjusted her glasses and eyed her reflection in the mirror. The wedding gown was gorgeous. A beaded bodice glimmered in the light and the full skirt flared at her hips. She'd left her hair loose and curly —the way Tucker liked it—but pulled a few tendrils into a clip so the veil had something to attach to. Butterflies flitted in her stomach. She could hardly believe the big day was finally here.

"You look stunning," Cassie said, clapping her hands together. Her eyes shimmered and her blonde locks were gorgeous against the deep-blue bridesmaid's gown.

"Absolutely." Kaylee used a tissue to pat the corners of each eye. "I don't think I've ever seen a more beautiful bride."

"Not true. Next month, it's your turn, and I'm positive you'll outshine me."

Leah smiled at her friend. Kaylee was engaged to Phillip. The couple had fallen more and more in love with every passing day, and it warmed Leah's heart to see Kaylee so happy.

Today, her cheeks glowed with health and vitality. Her hair was cut in an adorable bob that framed her face. She'd gained at least twenty pounds since being rescued and rediscovered her laugh. Leah and Kaylee had spent a lot of time together in the aftermath of Holt's arrest. Their bond was stronger than ever. Last month, for William's birthday, they'd gone to his grave for a visit. Kaylee's twin would never be forgotten.

The door to the dressing room opened and Mimi walked in. She wore a beautiful silver gown that fluttered around her calves. The wellness center had done her a world of good. She'd recommitted to her faith, started a new career at a local daycare, and moved into a small house in town.

Mimi and Leah had also worked hard to repair their relationship. Her mother was incredibly supportive and joyful. They finally had the mother-daughter bond Leah had always prayed for.

God, it seemed, had answered all her prayers. Leah was officially cured of cancer. Her oncologist had wanted to meet in person to give the good news. Five years in remission meant the chances of it ever returning were slim. Leah was incredibly grateful, but also knew in her heart that Tucker would stand by her even if it came back.

Mimi caught sight of Leah and gasped. "Oh, honey, you look gorgeous." She clapped her hands together. "It's time to start the ceremony. Are you ready?"

Leah nodded. She wanted to soak every second of this in. Marrying the man of her dreams was a fairy tale come true.

A group was gathered in front of the doors that led to the church interior. Logan, handsome in his tux, held out his arm to Mimi. "Mother of the bride, we're up."

Mimi lightly kissed Leah's cheek before taking his arm. They went around the corner and disappeared inside the church.

Walker was also dressed in a tux but had paired it with cowboy boots. He held Jax's and Coconut's leashes. The dogs each wore an outfit for the occasion—Jax, a bow tie, and Coconut, a cute little blue dress. They wriggled with excitement but obediently followed Walker into the church. Cheers and exclamations of joy erupted from the guests.

Kaylee followed on Jason's arm. Cassie was paired with her husband, Nathan. As the couple disappeared into the church, Leah's heart raced.

Nelson offered her his arm. The diner's chef looked so different in his tux. Tears shimmered in his eyes. Underneath his hard exterior, he'd always been a softy. When Leah had asked him to give her away, he'd cried like a baby. It'd moved her deeply. She considered Nelson and Harriet to be her surrogate grandparents.

"Ready, darlin'?" Nelson asked.

Leah took a deep breath and slid her hand in the crook of his arm. "Ready."

The wedding march played. Leah took several steps forward, and then suddenly she was in the church. A collective gasp arose from the guests. Chief Garcia was there with his wife. Addison and Sierra were sitting together in the front. Sierra's nephew, Daniel, looked adorable in his suit. Harriet was with them. She dotted at her eyes with a lace handkerchief.

And then Leah's gaze landed on Tucker. Her breath caught. He stood tall and proud in his tux at the altar. His beard was neatly trimmed and his auburn hair gleamed in the lights. If his flushed cheeks were any indication, Tucker was fighting back his emotions. Tears filmed his gorgeous eyes.

Their gazes met and the rest of the world fell away. All of Leah's nerves settled.

She took a step forward. And then another.

Straight toward the man she loved.

ALSO BY LYNN SHANNON

Texas Ranger Heroes Series

Ranger Protection

Ranger Redemption

Ranger Courage

Ranger Faith

Ranger Honor

Ranger Justice

Triumph Over Adversity Series

Calculated Risk

Critical Error

Necessary Peril

Strategic Plan

Covert Mission

Tactical Force

Would you like to know when my next book is released? Or when my novels go on sale? It's easy. Subscribe to my newsletter at www. lynnshannon.com and all of the info will come straight to your inbox!

Reviews help readers find books. Please consider leaving a review at your favorite place of purchase or anywhere you discover new books. Thank you.